POISON BERRY

NIGHTGARDEN SAGA #3

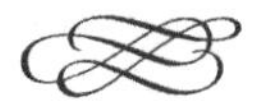

LUCY HOLDEN

For Suzanne and Noreen, the legendary ladies of the Pool Book Club.

PROLOGUE

Dear Tessa,

I'm writing this in the garden I made by the river, as the night jasmine opens beneath the stars. You gave me the seeds just before you went to the hospital for the last time. You told me to plant them when I found a place to call home. Two weeks ago, the night after Cass became a vampire, I mixed the last of your ashes with the seeds and put them in my night garden, here at the mansion.

You always said I could make anything grow. After you died, though, I stopped gardening. Something in me didn't feel able to put my hands in soil, cultivate anything. I think I was terrified of growing something, only to watch it die. I couldn't bear any more death.

That has changed since we came here.

Now, I'm learning to accept death, to live with it. To understand that even in death, there is life; that in the most toxic of plants, there is a gift. Night jasmine is poisonous, and yet it is a secret, exotic delight. I refuse to fear death anymore. My night garden is how I survive the long hours when Antoine is gone, Connor is God alone knows where, and my beautiful friend

Cass is out there somewhere, lost in the darkness. My night garden is where I go to restore my own soul, to feel the warm river earth beneath my fingers and reassure myself that somehow, we will survive all of this.

I know Antoine loves me. He can't hide that anymore, and it is a miracle no less than the flowers that open beneath the moon that he feels even part of what I do for him. But even love will not keep him at my side when this is over, and Cass is rescued. In the moments we are together I forget Cass, I forget everything. I feel guilty that I can be so happy when so much is crumbling around us.

None of us have seen Cass since the day she was made, though we've heard plenty. She has joined Keziah and Caleb, the vampires who spent the past three hundred years bound in the cellar of the Marigny mansion. Now the binding that held them captive is broken. The trio crossed the river into Louisiana the day Cass was made. Since then, they've cut a bloodthirsty swathe through the riverside towns, leaving a trail of unsolved murders and drained bodies in their wake. The nightly news has begun to talk about "deadly gang wars" and "strange cult rituals."

The only thing holding them in check is the newborn wolf pack from the bayou, led by Remy. The bite from a wolf must be dangerous even to Keziah, because she runs from their scent. The pack roam the perimeter of the bayou towns, trying to protect as much ground as possible. Without their presence, I suspect the news would have a lot more bodies to talk about.

Despite what the wolves report, I can't equate the sweet, quiet Cass who has been my friend since I came to Deepwater with the fierce monster everyone's talking about. I'm not blind to what she is now. I saw the savagery in her face after Antoine worked the sun magic into her body. I just think there's more to what she is than the monster they talk of, is all.

Antoine blames himself for what she has become. He and

Tate have tried to track Keziah, but Antoine says she knows all too well how to hide, even from him, whom she made. Keziah doesn't summon him anymore. Antoine says that's because now she has Cass, a tool she can wield at her own pleasure.

Connor is devastated by Cass's transformation. He blames himself as much as Antoine does, I think. But he doesn't speak of it, and whatever self-recrimination he suffers doesn't go any way to making him excuse Antoine's part. He can barely look at Antoine or me. Connor spends his nights driving the backroads of Louisiana, hoping, I guess, for a glimpse of the girl he loves, a chance to bring her home.

None of us have the heart to say the obvious—that even if by some miracle he's able to convince Cass to leave Keziah's side, she can never truly return. She will never be the schoolgirl she once was, planning college and a career. This transformation isn't some phase that will pass. Cass is a vampire. It isn't something that can be undone.

Keziah has compelled Selena, Cass's mom, to believe that Cass has gone to a music camp over in Biloxi for the spring semester. Keziah has done a good job. Selena is excited and happy for Cass, and not at all bothered by her daughter's lack of communication.

Avery, too, blames herself for being the means by which Keziah broke out of the cellar. She's been trying to understand more about the power of her Natchez blood, and how she might use it, rather than have it used against her. Connor still won't speak to her. He won't speak to me, either. I don't know that he will ever forgive me for all the secrets I kept—especially the secret of my marriage to Antoine.

The nights are the hardest. Antoine and Tate roam far and wide in search of Cass. Connor does the same. And I wait at home, with only the distant howls of the wolves as comfort.

That's why I created a night garden. Planted in a half circle around a small pond, I filled it with seeds that grow only at night. Many of them are toxic, but that doesn't stop them from being unutterably beautiful. I planted your seeds here. The books say jasmine blooms only in summer, but barely a week passed before the first flower burst open under the stars. Now their heady scent wends among the moonvine and magnolias like a sensual dream. They thrive and blossom, defying death, just as we do.

All I can do is hold on to the moments we have and try not to imagine the desert my life will be when Antoine is no longer here. Every time he leaves I can't help but feel he is preparing for a more final goodbye. I know that's why he doesn't spend his nights here, why he pulls away from me when I would pull him down onto my bed. He still holds on to the dream that I can have a normal life, one without a vampire husband and wolves over the river.

For now, he has not annulled our marriage. For now, I am Harper Marigny, with the Marigny emerald on my wedding finger and a husband I love more than I ever dreamed possible.

You and I know happiness is fleeting, Tessa. I have to grasp it while Antoine is here—even if I do so while Connor is suffering, and Cass has become something we don't recognize.

The night jasmine is bursting into life under the new moon, and the red magnolias lie in a crushed carpet under my bare feet.

I am alive. I am loved. This is what I know.

Sometimes it seems I hear you, whispering on the wind. I feel you here, Tessa. In the earth. In the trees.

With me.

YOUR TWIN,

Harper

CHAPTER 1

MARRIAGE

I wake to an engine in the driveway and voices murmuring in the kitchen. I lie in bed for a moment and savor the comforting sound of Antoine and Tate talking in the kitchen as they make coffee. I know they won't come upstairs. Tate respects my privacy, and Antoine, I suspect, doesn't trust himself anywhere near my bedroom. That thought should make me smile, but it doesn't.

Despite the fact that Antoine has barely left my side in the two weeks since Cass was made, I'm uncomfortably aware that he never allows himself to lose control with me. With the binding broken, there's no reason for Antoine and me to remain married. Keziah and Caleb are no longer held captive by the title deed to the mansion, and so there's no need for my name to be Marigny. Our marriage could be annulled today, the work of an instant.

I try to push the unsettling thoughts from my mind, smiling at the comforting chatter below. The smile fades after my shower, when I'm pulling on denim shorts and a cotton top, listening out for Connor's voice. As usual, it isn't there. I put my head around his door just to check. If the dirty clothes left on his bedroom floor are any indication, he returned yesterday when I was at school to wash and change, then left again. His work on both the mansion and his construction business has come to an abrupt halt since Cass was turned, and I've barely seen him. His absence makes me feel like part of myself is missing. Connor is the only family I have left. The thought of life without him in it is too cold and lonely to even imagine.

I swallow my disappointment and walk downstairs to find Antoine and Tate leaning against the peeling Ionic columns on the porch, sipping coffee in companionable silence. Since the night of Cass's transformation, an odd truce seems to have developed between them, albeit an unspoken one. The thought of either of them opting for a serious heart-to-heart discussion of their emotions is enough to make me actually smile. Whether it's a product of the era in which they were born or just their natures, two men less inclined to soul baring I can't imagine.

"I'm glad we amuse you." Antoine tugs gently at one of the flyaway curls bursting from the copper pile on my head. "What exactly is holding all that up?"

"A strategically placed pencil." I reach for the coffee, passing by a little closer than I need to. His eyes narrow. I feel the giddy rush of power I'm still not accustomed to, a thrill at the knowledge that he wants me. Perhaps not as much as I do him, but enough, at least, that he finds my nearness disturbing.

Tate is smirking into his coffee. I turn away to hide the color in my face.

"You didn't find Cass, did you." I sip my coffee, my words a statement rather than a question.

"No." Antoine's reply is equally terse.

Every morning I ask the same thing. Every morning Antoine has the same answer.

"What about Connor?" I try to keep my voice even. This time there is a short pause, then Tate answers.

"No, Harper. We didn't see Connor."

We didn't see Connor. Not "didn't find" Connor, I note. *Didn't see.* It's a slight difference, but one I notice, just as I notice that every morning it is Tate who answers that particular question, not Antoine.

They know where my brother is. They just won't tell me. And Antoine can't bring himself to actually lie to me, so Tate does it for him.

Every day we all pretend these exchanges are normal, because right now all we have is the illusion of normalcy to cling to, and sometimes, I guess, a lie or two is a small price to pay to maintain the fiction.

"Well—I'd better go." Tate pushes off the column and heads out to his truck, pretending not to notice the high color on my face, or my lack of invitation to stay for breakfast. He swapped out his flashy rental convertible for an old pickup a couple of days after Cass left. I take that to mean he plans to stay in Deepwater awhile. "Things to do," he says as he opens the truck door, but I see the flash of a crooked smile as he climbs inside and pulls away.

I can almost feel Antoine's storm-tossed eyes on my back. "Do you want some pancakes before I go?" I try to keep my voice steady. "I can mix some up—" I don't get any further before Antoine's arm snakes around my waist, pulling me back against him. "I don't want pancakes." He reaches up and plucks the pencil from my hair, sending the mass of curls tumbling chaotically down my back as he turns me to face him.

"That's better." His hand twines in my hair and his mouth is on mine, and it's lucky I already put my coffee cup down, because I can't tell what way is up anymore. One large hand is splayed at the base of my spine, and there is only denim and thin cotton between him and me. His mouth moves away and I press against him, my lips on his neck, and then he puts his head back and takes a deep breath, his hands slipping down to hold me loosely by the hips, putting an unwelcome distance between us. My body arches toward him as if it has a will of its own. "Come upstairs."

He ducks his head in a reluctant negative. "I can't, Harper." He strokes the hair down my back. "We can't."

"Yes, we can." I hide my face against his neck. "We're married."

I've never dared say it aloud before. I feel him tense against me, then his jaw hardens as he turns away.

"We need to go. You'll be late to class." His tone is slightly rough. I can feel the tension in his body, the stillness of the hands that only a moment ago roamed freely all over me. "Get your things." He's out of reach now. "I'll drive. And take something to eat on the way."

When I come back out from the kitchen, Antoine has his hands on his hips, feet apart, staring moodily down the slope toward the night garden.

"The plants are starting to bloom already," I say.

"It's the middle of winter. Those magnolia trees shouldn't have flowers." He glares at them accusingly.

"Things just seem to grow here." I put my bag over my shoulder. I don't mention Tessa's ashes in the soil, or my fanciful belief that my twin somehow talks to me through the trees and plants here. We have enough crazy around us without my imagination taking hold.

"I haven't felt like painting, lately." I glance guiltily at the library where my half-finished mural lies abandoned on one wall. I can't so much as bring myself to look at it. All I can think of when I do is Cass's lifeless body lying on the floor beneath it. "Gardening is what I'm doing instead."

Our eyes meet for a moment, and Antoine's soften. He puts his arm around me, and I lean against his comforting strength as we go toward his truck.

Halfway into Deepwater, the sun is gleaming off the slow,

brown river when I speak again. "The Legacy Committee's Midwinter Ball is in a few weeks."

"A bit late, isn't it? Midwinter was a fortnight ago."

I shrug. "I guess they can't hold a ball during the holidays." I take a breath. "Would you go with me?"

He shoots me a quizzical glance. "A ball, Harper?"

"Connor is their grant winner for this year. He's supposed to be the guest of honor. I know he was going to take Cass. Now . . . well, I guess we both know that isn't possible. I can make up some excuse for Connor. But one of us should go. It's expected." I look out the window to hide the color in my face. "I'd like it if you came with me."

When I look back, Antoine's smile has gone and he's shaking his head. "That isn't a good idea, Harper."

My heart sinks. "Why not?" Perhaps it's the recollection of his earlier lack of control, but I feel a little reckless, tired of all that lies unspoken between us. "What are you so afraid of, Antoine?"

He doesn't answer until we pull into the lot at school. He gets out of the truck and slams his door with unnecessary force, then comes around and wrenches mine open. I stand up, fold my arms and meet his hard stare with my own. "Well?"

"Three hours ago, Harper, what do you think I was doing?" He puts one hand on the truck behind me. I'm leaning against it, and he is so close I can inhale the cedar scent of him. It makes my senses whirl.

"I don't know." I try to shrug.

"Then let me tell you." He leans forward, and despite the fact that we are in a public lot, my body is already reacting to his nearness, swaying toward him, and I catch my breath as he puts his mouth so close to my ear I can feel the touch of his lips on my skin. "Three hours ago," he murmurs, "I was compelling a drunken man outside a roadhouse to let me drink his blood, and then to forget he'd ever seen me. When I'd finished with him, I was still thirsty, so I found a woman who was sad and tired and had nowhere to go, and then I drank from her. A few hours from now she will wake to find herself in a cheap motel with fifty dollars she didn't know she had, a little dizziness, and a strange resolution that she never wants to drink alcohol again. That's what I was doing three hours ago, Harper, while you were sleeping in your bed and dreaming of midwinter balls." He pulls back and his eyes are dark steel on mine. "Now do you see why going to a ball with me is a bad idea?"

I feel the intensity of his words, the dark scenes they evoke. My hands go up to hold his face. "You say those things as if they should scare me." I search his eyes. "But you drank from me, remember? I'm not afraid of you, Antoine. I'm not frightened by what you do to survive."

"You should be." He steps back, taking my hands from his face and holding them in his own. "What we do to exist isn't a game, Harper. Even if I have sworn never to drink from you again, you need to know that. To really understand what it means."

I frown, about to say it was my choice to give him my blood, one I would make again, when a sharp voice interrupts us.

"Miss Ellory. The school parking lot is not a nightclub." It's Mr. Larkin, the tightly buttoned history teacher, and he's glaring at Antoine and I as if we were naked and horizontal. Avery and Jeremiah are standing behind him, openly laughing at us.

"I'm sorry, Mr. Larkin." Aware that half the lot is watching, I step away from Antoine, who is looking at Mr. Larkin with a half smile and folded arms, as if daring the teacher to say something else.

"I'll pick you up this afternoon, Harper." He's loud enough to be heard by the entire lot.

"Hmph." Mr. Larkin glares at him. "I hardly think Harper's

brother would approve of someone your age collecting her from class, Mr—"

"Marigny," Jeremiah interjects, grinning. "Antoine Marigny is my guardian, Mr. Larkin."

"Your guardian?" Mr. Larkin looks Antoine up and down disapprovingly, taking in the faded jeans, loose linen shirt, and insolent grin. "You're a little young to be a guardian, don't you think, Mr. Marigny?"

Antoine cocks his head at the teacher. "Well, now that's funny. Weren't you just saying I was a little too old to be collecting Harper from class?" Raising his eyebrows quizzically, Antoine moves around to the driver's side door. Then he pauses and turns back. A moment later his mouth is on mine, hard and deep enough to set my skin aflame and make every kid in the parking lot hoot and whistle. When he finally pulls back, he grins down at me. "Behave." He nods at Mr. Larkin. "And you be certain to have yourself a nice day, now." Swinging himself into the truck, he murmurs, "I've never been great at authority." He pulls out of the lot with a jaunty wave, leaving a glowering Mr. Larkin in his wake as he drives away.

I walk inside between Avery and Jeremiah, a warm feeling in my chest. Mr. Larkin follows us, still glaring over his shoulder at the dust haze left by my husband's truck.

CHAPTER 2

MONSTERS

"Way to be subtle," says Avery on the way to history, but she's smiling. It's good to see her smile. Lately all I've seen are furrowed brows and worry. "So you and Antoine are pretty serious, huh?"

I make a noncommittal sound and look studiously ahead. She casts an assessing eye over the knotted mass of hair falling down my back and my flushed face. "Uh huh. So have you slept with him yet?"

"Avery!" I'm going for shocked, but it's Avery, so she just raises her eyebrows and waits for an answer.

"No." I stare at the floor, my face flaming for the second time that morning.

"Why not?" She gives me side eye. "You're married, aren't you?"

"Avery!" This time I'm not faking the shock. I drop a book and look around to see if anyone heard her. "It's more complicated than that," I hiss.

"Is it?"

I can feel her eyes on my back as I pick the book up, and I'm glad when Mr. Larkin passes by, glaring at us both. I scurry inside and take my seat, which is thankfully out of Avery's line of sight. I don't know how to answer her questions. I don't understand the answers to them myself.

Jeremiah leans over the aisle. "Don't mind Avery. She's still getting used to . . ." his eyes drop to the emerald on my finger. "You know."

"Oh, I know," I mutter. Avery's not the only one getting used to it. I just don't want the entire senior class to be getting used to it, as well.

The class is still clattering books and pens when the door opens again, and an odd silence falls across the room.

"What the actual French toast," hisses Jeremiah beside me.

I look up and freeze.

Standing in the doorway, looking like three improbably perfect models dropped from a Parisienne catwalk, are Keziah, Cass, and Caleb.

Only, the gleaming, glamorous figure standing between the other two isn't the Cass I knew. And by the shocked expressions on the faces of the rest of the class, it isn't the Cass they remember.

I don't think she's actually taller than she was. Perhaps it's her slick braids that make it seem that way, coiled into an intricate crown that towers high on her head. Or maybe it's the black silk dress she wears, dropping in sheer perfection to mid-gleaming-thigh. No—it's the heels, I realize. All sleek six inches of them. Nobody wears heels like that to school. Before today, I don't think I've ever seen Cass wear heels at all. Or, a silk dress, for that matter. The diamond and gold thread earrings falling down her neck look real, as does the matching ring on her hand. But it's really her eyes that stand out.

The last time I saw them they were bloodred, fierce and strange, the eyes of a predator. I'm not sure what she's done to tame them, but now they are the gleaming, savage gold of a great cat. They look disdainfully across the classroom, passing over both Avery and me as if we weren't there at all. Perhaps it's my growing familiarity with supernatural creatures that makes me notice the shimmering, shifting light in their depths, a strange iridescence, like an oil slick on water. Antoine's is purple and gold, like sun behind clouds, where Cass's gleam crimson and gold, like mixed metals.

"Mr. Larkin?" Keziah's voice sends a shiver down my spine. It's familiar from the long-ago dreams when she sought access to my mind, with a faint accent that I can't quite place, and a certain old-fashioned cadence that, given her age, is unsurprising. "The registrar sent us here. I'm Keziah Joseph, and this is my brother, Caleb. We're Cass's cousins. She's been visiting with us in Biloxi for a time."

"Ah." Mr. Larkin is still staring at Cass as if she's dropped in from Mars. "Miss Charles. I had been informed you would be away for the entirety of the spring semester, but never mind. It looks like the dress code in Biloxi was rather more—relaxed, than here in Deepwater. Perhaps you might like to revisit the regulations regarding the appropriate skirt lengths." His eyes flicker from Cass to Keziah, who is regarding him with faint amusement. Her hair is wound into a complex bun high on her crown, pieces falling artfully about her face, and she wears an electric-blue woollen dress that plunges so low at her cleavage that every boy in class can't seem to move their eyes from the deep-gold flesh swelling above it. Beside her, Caleb's shirt opens a button too low, exposing a chest hard and muscled enough to have the girls sitting up a little straighter. His sloping eyes are dark and watchful over high, flat cheekbones and a wide nose, and he doesn't smile at all. His skin is the colour of polished mahogany, as if a dull red shines somewhere deep inside. The effect is both startling and lethal.

Mr. Larkin clears his throat and frowns at Cass. "It seems your cousins, also, may need to learn that they are no longer in Biloxi. Deepwater Hollow is a small town, Miss Charles, and as

I mentioned earlier to your friend Miss Ellory, this school is not a nightclub. Please take a seat."

He turns away before he sees the way the three glide into their seats, their movements so nonchalantly preternatural that I stifle a gasp, certain others must have noticed. The glamorous appearance of the stunning trio, however, has so gripped the class that their inhuman swiftness seems to pass unnoticed.

"If that's what happens after two weeks in Biloxi," murmurs a girl behind me, "take me now."

"Never knew Cass Charles had those legs," says Jared Baudelaire to his friend. "Might have to tap that."

"As if you'd have a chance," his friend hisses back, "with Denzel Washington there as competition. I'm going to try for the other cousin, though. She is smoking hot."

"My man." They high five.

I tune them out and stare at the back of Cass's head, my heart beating a rapid tattoo. Jeremiah and Avery are trying to catch my eye. I have no idea what to do.

"As I was saying yesterday," drones Mr. Larkin, "the Natchez nation was largely dispersed after the 1729–32 war with the French settlers, with many being sent to work as slaves on plantations in the Caribbean. Yes, Miss Fairweather?" He says Avery's name with distaste as he eyes her over his glasses.

"Not all the Natchez were dispersed then, Mr. Larkin. I was wondering what you might know about the rumors of another tribe, on the Louisiana side of the river."

"She means the wolves," says Jared derisively from behind me. The boys around him all hoot, making faux wolf howls.

"Thank you, Mr. Baudelaire." Mr. Larkin shoots Jared a quelling stare. "Yes, Miss Fairweather, we've all heard the recent rumors about wolves in the bayou. However, no matter how you might enjoy the legends associated with your people, I can assure you nobody in Deepwater Hollow is turning into a wolf under a full moon. This is not Forks, Washington, and you, Miss Fairweather, are not Bella Swan."

There is a good-natured outburst of laughter at this, through which Keziah's voice cuts like a knife.

"Perhaps not, Mr. Larkin. However, as I'm certain a man of your knowledge is aware, there was a massacre on the Louisiana side of the river, in 1732. One attributed to a band of renegade Natchez—whom legend has it could turn themselves into wolves." Mr. Larkin is looking at her, and with a sinking feeling I recognize the slightly dazed expression in his eyes as he starts to nod at her words: Keziah is compelling him. "Isn't it true, Mr. Larkin," Keziah's high, clear voice goes on, "that the version of history you teach in this class is one made up by white bigots such as yourself, and in fact bears not the vaguest resemblance to what actually occurred?"

Mr. Larkin is not known for his tolerance. The class stirs, tittering nervously, waiting for the teacher to explode. Even Mr. Larkin's temper, however, is no match for an ancient vampire with exceptional powers of mind control.

"I suppose, when you put it like that, Miss Joseph," he says, in a slightly bewildered tone, "you do make a good point."

"Oh, Mr. Larkin." Keziah leans forward, giving the teacher the full benefit of her deep cleavage. "I'm sure you understand my points very well." Now the class gasps at her audacity, looking at each other wide-eyed. "In fact," Keziah goes on, and now Mr. Larkin is clearly entirely hypnotized by her voice, "I think you were just about to concede that you know so little, your class would be better served by leaving early and doing independent research."

"No way," breathes someone behind me, but Mr. Larkin is already nodding.

"Yes, Miss Joseph. I can see how that would be helpful." He looks vacantly around at the rest of us. "Class, please use the rest of this period to do as Miss Joseph suggests. Research the colonial and Native American wars of 1729–32 as you see fit."

"Why, thank you, Mr. Larkin," says Keziah, standing up gracefully. "And if any of you would like to join us"—she flashes a beaming smile around the room that is so seductive the boys are almost knocking each other over in their haste to reach her —"I promise, we know how to have a good time."

She may say more, but I don't hear it, because the sound of clattering chairs and escaping students is deafening.

Avery, Jeremiah, and I are left staring at each other in a classroom empty but for a bewildered Mr. Larkin.

"What the hell are they doing here?" hisses Jeremiah.

"Mr. Marigny!" Mr. Larkin seems to have collected himself in Keziah's absence and is glaring at us. "I suggest you and your friends go and do the research I asked you to, rather than sit here idly gossiping."

"Oh, really," says Avery sarcastically as we stand up. "And what was that research exactly, Mr. Larkin?"

"Avery!" I shoot her a warning glance and pull her away before she can do more damage. Poor Mr. Larkin looks utterly bewildered by her question. Even if he isn't exactly my favorite teacher, nobody deserves to be compelled by the likes of Keziah. "What are you doing?" I say, noticing Jeremiah pulling out his phone as we leave the classroom.

"Texting Antoine. He and Tate need to know what's going on."

"Don't." I put my hand over his phone, and Jeremiah frowns at me.

"Why not?"

Because Antoine will go nuclear, I want to say. Because it will be just more evidence that his presence in my life is dangerous. Because selfishly, I don't want to do anything that might shake the fragile bliss of the precious days we have together.

I'm saved from having to find a good reason by the sudden,

devastating appearance of Cass, standing right in front of us, her expression remote and hostile. "Don't do anything stupid," she says coldly, glancing at the phone in Jeremiah's hand. "Keziah won't like it if you call Antoine—or Tate."

"What do we care what Keziah will like?" Jeremiah shoots back at her. "We aren't her little minions."

"Jeremiah." I shake my head at him. "Cass," I say gently. "Are you okay?"

The crimson and gold eyes shift to me, her mouth curling contemptuously. "Harper," she says, as if remembering me after a long absence. "Still to discover what a hairbrush is for, I see." She slides her gaze right, to Avery, and although I didn't think her expression could get any colder, it does. "I'd stop playing around with Natchez magic, if I were you," she says scornfully. "You don't have the brains to understand it or the power to wield it."

Avery swallows hard. "I'm so sorry, Cass," she says hesitantly. "For what I did to you."

"Don't be." Cass is smiling again, but there is no warmth in it, only chilling contempt. "I'm better this way. I'm strong now."

"But you can't stay here, Cass." I take a hesitant step toward her, trying to suppress my own trepidation. "You're putting everyone in danger."

Cass raises perfectly arched eyebrows disdainfully. "Keziah likes it here," she says. "She wants to go to high school. I've been teaching her about the modern world. Did you know she was only seventeen when she was turned? Last time she was here, girls like her were no more than playthings for white men. Now those men are *our* playthings." She smiles at me, that same cold, assessing smile. "Just as all humans are playthings to us, Harper. Including you." She takes a step closer, and I have to make a conscious effort to remain still as she leans in and takes a deep breath, as if she is inhaling me. "Mm," she murmurs. "I see why Antoine is so protective of you."

I can't suppress a shudder. "What about Selena, Cass?" I try to keep my voice steady. "What are you going to tell your mother?"

She shrugs carelessly. "Selena has been compelled. If she causes trouble, Keziah will kill her, I guess. What does it matter?"

"What does it matter?" Avery looks at her incredulously. "You love your mother, Cass. You adore her. This isn't you. I don't believe you are just gone. This is Keziah's mind control."

Suddenly Avery is slammed up against the lockers, her feet off the ground, Cass holding her by the neck with one careless, preternaturally strong hand. "Just because you were weak enough to be Keziah's servant, Avery, don't make the mistake of thinking me so pathetic." Even her voice sounds different, the cadence and structure more Keziah's than Cass's customary informal speech. "I love Keziah. She is my Maker. I owe her everything. And my mother—ha." Cass laughs mirthlessly. "She's food, just as you are. Humans exist to be enjoyed. You don't matter, do you understand? None of you matter at all. We will stay as long as we choose. We will do as we wish. And if any of you have a brain at all, you will stay out of our way." She drops Avery to the floor and turns to me. "And you, Harper, are the stupidest of all." Her eyes gleam with hostility. "You still believe Antoine is with you because he actually loves you."

Before I can ask what she means, she is gone. We're left standing in the hallway, Avery pale-faced and clutching her throat, all of us staring silently after the monster who used to be Cass, our friend.

CHAPTER 3

TUMBLING

"I'm calling Antoine." Jeremiah has his phone out again.

"Jeremiah, no. Please, let's just wait a little."

"He has to know sooner or later, Harper." It's Avery, her voice uncharacteristically gentle as she puts a hand on my arm. "The longer we wait the more dangerous it is, for everyone."

"I know that. But please." I look pleadingly at Jeremiah. "Just give me an hour or so, to work out what they're doing here."

"Cass was pretty clear on that," Jeremiah says grimly. "Sounds like they plan to make Deepwater High their own personal playground. The sooner Antoine and Tate get here, the sooner we can make people safe."

"Safe?" I roll my eyes. "What do you think will happen when Antoine and Tate get here, Jeremiah? Our entire school could end up a bloodbath. Do you really want that?"

Jeremiah makes an impatient sound. "Have you got a better idea, Harper? Because I sure didn't see Cass paying you any mind when you tried talking to her. And what did she mean about Antoine, and about you being stupid, anyhow?"

"I have no idea. More of Keziah's mind games, I guess." In fact, I can't stop thinking about what Cass said, but I don't intend to let Jeremiah know that. "Just give me an hour to try to talk to her. Then you can call Antoine, I promise."

Jeremiah shakes his head. "This is a bad idea."

"But we have to try," says Avery. I shoot her a grateful glance and she gives me a rueful smile. "It's Cass, Jeremiah. Our friend is still in there, somewhere."

"I'm not so sure about that," mutters Jeremiah, but Avery's long eyelashes clearly still hold some power over him, because he backs off. "One hour," he says grudgingly. "But after that I'm calling Antoine, no matter what either of you say. And we're sticking together until then."

"Well, that means you're going to have to actually attend gym class for once," I say. "That's where Cass is now."

Jeremiah rolls his eyes. "Great," he mutters resignedly. "This day just keeps getting better." Jeremiah is one of the least coordinated people to ever enter a gymnasium. He has managed to avoid attending a class ever since I've been in Deepwater. Now he hugs his books protectively against his tall, awkward frame and reluctantly follows in our wake.

We reach the gym to find Keziah, Cass, and Caleb clad in uniforms that seem molded to their perfect bodies. "Is that a vampire thing?" Avery hisses in my ear. "The stunning looks, I mean? I swear Cass never had legs like that before." An unwelcome vision of Antoine's hard, sculpted perfection passes over my mind, causing me to temporarily lose focus.

"I guess so."

"Ha." Avery takes in my flaming face and shoots me a knowing glance.

"What is she doing?" Jeremiah is staring at the sprung floor in the middle of the gym, where Cass is surrounded by an admiring group of onlookers.

We edge closer in time to hear Miss Bowden, the gym teacher, say doubtfully, "Cass, I don't know that you've had enough experience to demonstrate that particular routine."

Given that Cass's gym attendance has been on par with Jeremiah's all year, the teacher's skepticism is well justified. Cheerleader material Cass most certainly isn't.

Up until now, at least, I mentally correct myself.

"Oh, I think you'll find I'm more than capable, Miss Bowden." Cass turns piercing eyes on the gym teacher, and instantly Miss Bowden's face takes on the familiar dazed, slightly bewildered expression of the compelled. I turn to find Keziah watching Cass with a satisfied smirk that makes me want to hit her across the room.

Cass glances briefly at Keziah, as if searching for approval, and when she receives a tiny nod of her Maker's head, looks like a dog who has just been given a treat.

"Seriously?" mutters Avery. For once, I find myself in total accord with her acidic asides.

Cass raises her arms to signify the start of a routine, then launches straight into a series of perfect backflips, culminating in a complex backwards tumble with a number of twists. She lands perfectly and arches her back in a proud gym salute, to the admiring cheers and whistles of the entire class. Beaming, Cass throws us a triumphant look over the heads of our classmates.

"Oh, for goodness' sake," groans Avery.

"Hey, Cass." It's Jared, pushing his way past us to Cass's side. "Want to show me some of those skills up close at lunch break?"

Cass shoots him a look hot enough to peel paint. "Well, sure, Jared," she says, her voice smooth as honey. "I'd love that."

"Cool." Looking satisfied with himself, Jared goes back to high-five his friends, oblivious to the predatory gleam in Cass's eyes as she watches him go.

"Oh, no," I say. "That isn't good."

Jeremiah raises his eyebrows at me. "Now can I call Antoine?"

"Just give me one moment." Cass is walking toward the changing rooms. Keziah is on the floor now, Caleb watching her with his arms folded, the rest of the class absorbed in what the new girl is doing.

"You can't follow her, Harper." Avery grips my arm. "Please don't follow her. Harper!"

I pull away. "Keep an eye on them."

"She's following her," Avery says resignedly behind me.

I enter the deserted changing room to find Cass waiting for me, fists tightly balled, eyes gleaming. She's both perfectly beautiful and utterly terrifying. "Don't you know when to give up?"

"What did you mean?" I force myself not to flinch from her. "When you said I was stupid to believe Antoine is in love with me?"

"Typical," she says scornfully. "Three vampires come to school, and all you care about is that emerald on your finger. You are possibly the most self-centered person I've ever met, Harper."

"And you're the cruelest." Goaded beyond fear, I glare at her. "Have you even thought about what you're doing to my brother? Connor hasn't slept since you left. He barely eats. He spends every waking moment searching for you, Cass. And all you can think of is showing off in gym class and seducing that idiot Jared Baudelaire, who you wouldn't have even looked at a month ago!"

Something flickers behind her eyes at the mention of Connor's name, an odd shadow in which I catch a glimpse of the girl I once knew. Then it is gone, and Cass throws me savagely against the locker. "I told you before," she hisses at me. "Don't get in my way. I've already told your brother to stop looking for me. Keziah doesn't like it."

"You've already told him?" I'm so taken aback I stop being afraid for a moment. "You mean you've seen Connor? Talked to him?"

Cass shakes me, her face hard. "Tell him I'm not coming back. Not ever. All of you need to understand that." She slams me so hard against the lockers that they shake. "This is how easy it is for me to end you." Lifting my arm with no more effort than if I were a rag doll, she slices it deliberately down the sharp edge of a locker door, deep enough that it leaves a long cut along my arm that instantly begins to drip blood. Cass inhales sharply, and for a moment the golden eyes gleam a deep, fierce crimson. "Let's see what your fake husband makes of that," she says.

Then she is gone.

A moment later Avery and Jeremiah burst through the door.

"What happened? We heard a crash, then Cass came out and her eyes were red, and then all three of them left—" Avery's eyes widen when she sees my arm. "Harper, your arm! What did she do to you?"

"That's it," says Jeremiah grimly, pulling out his phone. "Now I'm definitely calling Antoine."

This time, I don't stop him.

CHAPTER 4

PUPPETS

It's lunch break when Antoine's truck hurtles into the lot. Jeremiah, Avery, and I are on a bench near the art hall. Antoine and Tate are across the lawn and in front of us before I've barely registered their arrival. Grim-faced, Antoine seizes my arm, which now sports a fetching white bandage, thanks to the school nurse. "What did she do to you?"

"I'm fine." I pull my arm back. "It's a scratch, nothing more."

"A scratch that almost needed stitches," says Jeremiah, ignoring my glowering expression.

"Show me." Antoine is already reaching for the edge of the bandage.

"It's nothing, really." But Antoine, staring at the livid gash on my arm, swears softly under his breath. He looks up at Tate. "Find them," he says curtly.

"You're too late," Jeremiah says, halting Tate's departure. "They left after gym class."

"I think Cass got thirsty," I say, a little wary of the deadly look on Antoine's face. "When she cut my arm, I saw her eyes change. After she saw the blood."

"You need to see a doctor." Antoine is still staring at the cut on my arm.

"The nurse said it doesn't need stitches."

"And I don't care what the nurse said. We're taking you to a doctor."

"Why don't you just give her some of your blood?" Jeremiah is rummaging around in his bag, so he misses the odd expression in Antoine's eyes.

"No," Antoine says briefly. He looks sharply at Tate. "And you won't give her yours, either." Before I have time to comment, Antoine goes on speaking to Tate. "One of us will need to be here at the school. All the time."

"I know," Tate says. "But how?"

Antoine glances at Mr. Larkin, who is glaring at us over his coffee cup from across the lawn. "What does he teach?"

"History. Very badly." I give him a wry smile and am relieved to see a slight softening in his eyes.

Antoine raises his eyebrows quizzically at Tate. "Isn't it fortunate, brother, that history is your specialist subject?" He tilts his chin in Mr. Larkin's direction. "I feel that the current teacher is about to discover other duties that require his attention."

"High school teaching, brother?" Tate gives Antoine a pained look. "You really do like to see me suffer." But he heads off nonetheless, shooting me a rueful smile as he goes, and a moment later Mr. Larkin's face crumples into dazed bewilderment before he nods vacantly and sets off toward his car, still holding the coffee cup.

"And the entire senior class thanks you," says Avery, watching him go.

"Am I the only one disturbed by the fact that we just compelled a teacher?" I say, looking around.

"It's Mr. Larkin." Jeremiah shrugs. "No qualms here. He's the worst teacher I've ever had." It's hard to argue with that. Despite my horror at seeing Keziah in class today, even I'd felt a sneaking satisfaction at seeing Mr. Larkin's bigotry and ignorance so brutally exposed.

"Jeremiah," says Antoine, "take Harper to the doctor. So much as a sniff of Keziah, Cass, or Caleb, and you call me straight away, do you understand?"

"Wait." I shake off Jeremiah's arm and look at Antoine. "What are you going to do?"

Antoine fixes me with a hard eye. "First, I'm going to try to understand why it was lunch time before you felt the need to tell me that Keziah was in your class." I color, but I don't look away. He shakes his head in exasperation. "Then I'm going to get Avery here to tell me everything that happened today. After that, I'll try to make a plan to prevent the entire student body of Deepwater High from becoming the next cable news headline."

"Can't you talk to her?" I ask. "Keziah? Just find out what it is that she wants here? Cass said she spent the last couple of weeks teaching Keziah about the 'modern world.' Surely there are other places Keziah would rather be than Deepwater Hollow, where she was trapped for three centuries?"

"Harper's right." Jeremiah looks at Antoine. "Can you do that? Talk to Keziah?"

"I know Keziah," says Antoine grimly. "Trust me when I say that my talking to her would only bring that cable news headline closer. You have no idea the bloodbath that will be unleashed if she thinks for even a moment that we intend to stand in the way of whatever she's doing here."

"I'm not going to the doctor," I say firmly. When he opens his mouth to argue, I shake my head. "I'm fine. And I'm safer here, with you and Tate, than I am out there."

"That's debatable." Something in Avery's voice makes us all pause. "They're back," she says, nodding across the playing field.

Antoine whirls around. The three vampires stand against the far end of the bleachers like perfect sculptures, staring at us. Even from this distance, I can tell Keziah is smiling. She wipes her mouth with a white cloth, slowly and deliberately. None of us miss the bright red stains when she brings it away from her mouth. A moment later, Miss Bowden, the gym teacher, emerges from behind the bleachers. She is wearing a scarf about her neck, and an all-too-familiar dazed expression. Keziah gives her a cute little wave as she passes, still smiling in our direction.

"They fed on her," breathes Avery. "On our *teacher.*"

"Better on her than us," says Jeremiah.

Antoine is still as the three vampires across the field, balled fists his only visible sign of tension. Even from a distance, I can see Keziah's lips moving. From the set, hard expression on Antoine's face, something tells me that he is perfectly able to hear whatever it is she's saying.

Then the three vampires are walking back into the school building, and Antoine's face as he turns is so closed and forbidding that even Avery takes an involuntary step backward.

"I have to go."

"You can't just leave while they're here," I say, staring at him. "What if they hurt someone?"

"They won't—so long as I leave." He puts his hands on my shoulders, and I can feel the tension in his grip. "I need to go and find your brother. Stay close to Tate." His eyes shift to Jeremiah. "Don't let her out of your sight."

Jeremiah nods, and before I have a chance to so much as comment, Antoine is gone, so fast I see a girl nearby look around in confusion. It isn't like Antoine to be so careless. Whatever the reason he's going in search of Connor, it must be urgent. I feel a rush of frustration that whatever is going on, Antoine seems determined to keep it from me.

I spend the rest of the afternoon oblivious to the instructions in my art class, mulling over all the things I don't understand. What Cass meant, for example, about me being stupid for believing Antoine loves me. Or what Keziah was saying to him across the field. And most of all, why Antoine seems so determined not to give me his blood.

The more I think on it all, the more puzzled I am. Keziah, Caleb, and Cass are fortunately in the science classes that I don't take, and I'm so deep in thought I have almost forgotten their presence until the final bell goes, and I walk outside art hall to find them barely ten yards away. Keziah smiles in the knowing, self-satisfied way that so annoyed me earlier in the day. She walks toward me with her hand possessively on Cass's shoulder, as if Cass is some kind of prize she has won in a game. One in which I, clearly, am considered the loser.

A moment later, Tate is standing beside me. "Don't move," he murmurs.

The trio saunter close enough for me to touch Keziah. She looks Tate up and down. "He destroyed your life," she says lightly, "and yet still you follow Antoine like a broken puppy." Her eyes shift to me, and the smile widens to a kind of triumph. "I control Antoine, you know," she says conversationally. "I always will."

Without waiting for a response, she walks on, carrying Caleb and Cass with her as if they are puppets on a string.

"Why does he never speak?" I mutter, looking at Caleb's back.

Tate looks at me. "You were just within touching distance of the most dangerous vampire I know," he says, shaking his head, "and that's what is worrying you?"

"Did he speak when you knew him before?" I answer his question with one of my own. The fact is that if I think about Keziah's control over Antoine, I feel so savagely furious I'm almost afraid of what I will do.

"No." Tate walks with me to the lot, where Jeremiah is waiting to drive us both back to the Marigny mansion. "Caleb was always her puppet. I don't know that I ever heard him say a word."

For the entire journey home, all I can imagine is Antoine looking at me with the same vacant, dumb stare as Caleb, forced to do Keziah's will. No matter what Antoine once said about me being the reason he managed to resist Keziah last time she summoned him, I suspect that with her so close, that remedy might not work a second time. The thought of him falling under her control terrifies me.

We pull up at the mansion and my heart skips when I see Antoine's truck parked beneath the red magnolia. I take the steps two at a time, hoping against hope I will find Connor with him, then deflate just as fast when I get inside and see Antoine's bleak face.

"You didn't find him, did you." It isn't a question, and when Antoine speaks it isn't to answer me, but to address Tate.

"We need to go."

"Go where?" I look between them, feeling a familiar sense of irritation. "What aren't you telling me? Whatever it is, I deserve to know. Connor is my only family. I'm worried about him."

"She's right, brother," says Tate quietly.

Antoine's mouth tightens. He looks away. I fold my arms and lean against the doorframe, my eyebrows raised, waiting for an answer.

"Connor is with the wolves." Antoine says it in a curt, clipped tone that tells me there is a world he isn't saying.

"The wolves? Connor is with Remy? Why?"

"I don't know." Antoine still won't look at me, and again there is something in his face that seems to speak to Tate in a language I don't understand.

"One of you needs to explain," I say, looking between them, but now I'm met with two carefully blank expressions.

"We need to go," says Antoine again, and this time Tate doesn't argue. "I promise I will bring your brother back, Harper."

Before I can argue, they are both gone, and I'm left in the kitchen with Jeremiah, staring after them in frustration.

CHAPTER 5

MOJITO

Jeremiah offers to stay, but I feel drained and annoyed, unequal to conversation even with him. "I'm sorry," I say as I walk him to his car. "I'm just so worried about Connor that I'm afraid I'm not very good company just now."

"It's okay." Jeremiah hugs me before he gets into the car, his thin shoulders feeling terribly vulnerable when he does. *Will he be next?* I can't help but think. Will Keziah simply torture us by taking everyone we care about, one by one? "I'm here if you need me," he says through the open car window. "And try not to worry about Antoine, Harper."

It's only as he is driving away that I realize I never mentioned worrying about Antoine. *Jeremiah is a good friend.* And a perceptive one.

I know I won't sleep. Instead I make myself a very large, very strong mojito, in a huge beer stein someone gave Connor as a going away present when we left Baton Rouge. I'm not much of a drinker, but I figure tonight I get a pass. I pull on my Ariats and take my drink down to the night garden. It's an unusually mild winter, a comfortable fifty-five degrees even after dusk, and clouds cover the sky like a layer of insulation. I'm still in the denim shorts I wore to school, with only a plaid shirt over my cami. I get warm when I garden anyway.

I take a long pull on the mojito and wince slightly at the strength in it, but if ever I needed a little numbing in my life, tonight is the time. I kneel down and start turning over soil, finding a comfort in the loamy feel of it under my fingers, and the reassuring sense of Tessa close by. "I don't know what to do about Connor." I speak aloud. "I'm scared that losing Cass is one loss too many, you know? He's always been so strong, Tessa. First with Mom, then you—then for me, too. Cass was like his reward, the piece of happiness he got to have all for himself, the one thing that brought him comfort and security. Now she's gone forever. I'm not sure he's ever coming back from this. And I don't know what there is for him to come back to."

I carry on turning soil and dividing the seedlings into small boxes, chattering away to Tessa as if she were truly here, listening as she always did when I needed to talk. The sliver of new moon amid the clouds slips behind the horizon as I work, and between the mojito, slow-moving river, the silent rush of bats overhead, and the warm earth under my hands, time slips away. When a faint shift in the air alerts me to the presence of someone else, I swing around, startled, straining to see through the starless night.

"I didn't mean to scare you." Even when Antoine comes to my side, the night dark is so thick I can barely make out his features. "I thought there was someone else here," he says, looking around. "It sounded like you were talking to someone."

"I buried the last of Tessa's ashes here, in the night garden." I turn away to wash the water from my hands, grateful the darkness hides the color on my face. "When I work, sometimes it feels like she's here with me."

Perhaps it is because I can't see his face that I'm more attuned to the sound of his voice, but I seem to hear a tension in it when he says, "You buried your sister's ashes here? In the earth?"

"Why? Have I done something wrong?"

"No, no. Of course not. I'm glad you have a way to remember her." His answer sounds just a little hasty, but before I can focus on it too much, he goes on: "I know I promised I'd bring Connor home. I will keep that promise, if it takes me all night to do it, but I needed to come and tell you not to wait up, Harper. It's not going to happen fast."

"Where is he?" I'm proud that my voice doesn't crack.

"He's with Remy and the wolves. He's been there every waking moment, driving around with them at night, following where they go." Antoine pauses. "He's in a bad way, Harper. I wish I could say different, but I can't. He's drinking a lot. Connor is angry, with me and Tate especially. He isn't in any mind to come with us. I've left Tate with him. Remy knows Connor can't carry on like this forever. He won't stop us from taking him by force if we have to. But if we can, I'd prefer him to come of his own accord. He already has enough reason to dislike me."

"And me," I whisper.

"Harper." Antoine tilts my chin up gently. He's so close the heat of his body warms my own, and I realize with a faint shiver that the night has grown cold. "Your brother loves you. It isn't you he's angry at, not really. It's the world, for taking Cass from him."

"But what if we can't get her back?" I rest my face in the comforting cradle of his palm. "Even if Cass somehow gets away from Keziah, she's changed, Antoine. I saw it in her face today. She isn't the girl who was once my friend."

"We all change, when we are made vampire. Give her time.

The girl you know is in there still, I promise. Changed, yes; but in essence, still herself."

"Are you?" My hand comes up to cover his own. "The same, in essence, as you once were?"

He pulls back, his hand sliding down my face, away from my own. "I barely remember who I was before," he says quietly. "It was a long time ago, Harper. I was human for less than twenty four years. I've been a vampire for nearly three hundred. I can no longer clearly recall what I was then, compared to what I am now."

"Maybe they're the same."

"Maybe." His voice leaves no doubt he thinks I'm wrong.

"Is that why wouldn't you give me your blood, earlier today?" I ask. "Or let Tate give me his? Because you don't truly know who you are, now?"

There's a silence during which I can tell he is considering how much to say. "I just want the truth, Antoine. I feel like there is so much you don't want to tell me. But I can handle it. I promise."

He makes a harsh sound, almost like a laugh, but with a hard, pained edge. "You've already had to handle more than I ever wanted for you." He takes a breath, and then exhales slowly. When he speaks again his voice is steady and detached.

"When a vampire gives a human their blood, it creates a bond. Not one as strong as between Maker and vampire, but a bond, nonetheless. They become joined, in subtle ways. The vampire can track the human, for example. Be aware of their location at any given time, if they choose to be alert to it. Sense when they are endangered or sad. And the human—" his voice breaks off, as if he is weighing his words carefully.

"And the human?" I prompt him. "What is it like for them?"

"Even after compulsion, they often feel connected to the vampire, for a while, at least." He speaks reluctantly, as if the words are being forcibly dragged from him. "The human might dream about the vampire, for example. Perhaps desire them. Become devoted to them, worshipful, almost. It is part of our power, one of the ways some vampires are able to keep entire stables of humans as their own personal blood banks, willing—eager even—to serve the object of their devotion by offering their blood." His voice is scornful with distaste.

"But you gave your blood to Avery." I'm trying to make sense of it. "When she was attacked by Keziah, you gave her your blood. She doesn't seem devoted to you like that, or— attracted to you." I'm glad once again for the darkness that hides my face.

"Avery is . . . different. She is Natchez, a distant descendant of the medicine woman who gave her life for mine. We already share blood."

"And Connor?"

"Connor feels the bond to me. And resents it, deeply. He's spent every minute trying to outrun me, and the pull he feels toward me. I think it's all but faded now, but he made no secret of how repugnant he found it. Not that I blame him."

Poor Connor. I wince. On top of everything else, he now also feels a connection with Antoine, the man who married his sister and destroyed his girlfriend's life.

I also have the annoying sense that Antoine still isn't telling me the entire truth.

"I wouldn't mind," I say carefully, even more grateful than before for the darkness, "if I drank—I mean if we had that kind of connection—I wouldn't mind," I end lamely, not having said what I mean at all.

He laughs low in his throat and steps forward, his arms coming about me. I move into his embrace with a rush of relief, wanting only to be close to him. "But I would," he says, his lips moving against my hair. "And selfishly, I couldn't bear for you to have that bond with anyone else. Definitely not with Tate."

"But why—" my voice breaks off again as I search for the right words.

"Why don't I want to have that bond with you?" He pulls back slightly, and now that he is so close, I can see the storm in his eyes again, feel the intensity as they search my face. "Because," he says, his voice low, "I need to know that this, what lies between us, is entirely of your own will, Harper. I don't ever want to wonder if it is my blood holding you to me, overriding your own will. I couldn't be with you like this if I suspected, even for a moment, that it was my blood keeping you here." He wraps my hair around his hand. "And besides," he says roughly. "We don't need blood to bind us, Harper. There is no bond in existence that could ever make me feel more for you than I already do."

I stand on my tiptoes and put my arms around his neck.

It starts off a gentle thing, a reassurance in the only way I know of that can say what I don't have the words for. "You taste like mint," he murmurs against my mouth, and I can tell he is smiling. A moment later, though, the heat between us that seems always to simmer just beneath the surface ignites. The mojito from earlier sets something in me adrift, wanting more.

Then his hands are in my hair and roaming the length of my body, pulling me hard into him, lifting me up onto the low bough of the magnolia tree. The bare skin of my leg is aflame where he folds it behind him, his fingers leaving a hot trail up my thigh to my hip, his thumb tantalizingly close to where I want it. My head goes back and the plaid shirt slides off one shoulder, taking the strap of my cami with it. His lips roam lower, and I'm biting my own to stop myself moaning aloud. Then he puts his head back and draws a deep, ragged breath, raking one hand through his hair.

"We need to stop," he says hoarsely.

"Why?" I push myself toward him. His eyes, black as the moonless night, drop to the flesh swelling over white lace.

"God, Harper." I can hear the longing in his voice. "If you only knew what I want to do to you . . ."

"Then do it. Please." I reach for him, but he's already stepping back, his hand slipping my shirt back onto my shoulder as he does. "I won't do this," he says, and despite the huskiness of his voice, I can hear the resolution in it also. "It's late, Harper. You need to get to bed—and I need to go and bring your brother home."

CHAPTER 6

POWERLESS

I don't sleep.

The night grows deep, the scent of night jasmine heavy on the air, and I wander the creaking corridors of the mansion, my body aflame. The buds of moonvine are shut tightly closed under the dark of the moon, just as, it seems, Antoine has closed himself to me.

Despite the night's cool, my skin feels hot and restless, retaining the memory of Antoine's touch, as if his lips burned their imprint upon it. I can still feel the rough magnolia branch beneath my legs.

I can't believe Antoine doesn't want me. I can feel his longing, in the craving of his mouth, the fierce surge of him against me. *Then why?* I think savagely, stalking across the kitchen floor. *Why won't he be with me?* Is it because he still wants to annul our marriage? To avoid that last step that will make the piece of paper real, that will truly bind us? It seems cruel that he would deny us both this, not even allowing me to be heard.

I wish I had more experience. The truth is that between first Mom dying, then Tessa, romance has never had much of a chance in my life. Not that I feel inclined to share my lackluster past with Antoine. Given how reluctant he seems to consummate our marriage, the last thing I want to do is give him yet another reason to stay away from me. I can't help but wonder, though, whether if I were more experienced, I might know a way to change his mind. I feel as if what I don't know—about Antoine, vampires, or love itself—is a mountain so great I have no chance to begin to understand it. I feel inadequate, awkward, and unbearably lost.

I'm barely aware of the sky lightening, until I realize the magnolia tree is no longer an amorphous blob, but a series of distinct branches, and that my eyes are tired and grainy from the long night. I go upstairs and stand under a hot shower, wishing I could at least feel tired enough to sleep, but instead horribly aware that I'm wound as tight as a wire fence.

When I turn the water off, I hear an engine on the main road. Pulling on my shorts and tank top, my hair wet down my back, I race downstairs in time to see Connor's truck pull in, Antoine's close behind. My sudden, overwhelming rush of relief disappears as quickly as it came when Connor almost falls out of the truck cab and stumbles up the stairs. He raises bloodshot, accusing eyes to mine, his breath so heavy with alcohol fumes it almost bowls me over. "Out of my way," he says thickly, swaying on his feet as he passes me.

I stare at his back as he goes to the refrigerator, unsure what to say. I've never seen Connor like this. Raised the child of an alcoholic father, he's always been a very moderate drinker—a few beers, no more. I think he was twenty-one before he even had a drink. Sure, that increased a little in the months after Tessa's death, and when we first came to Deepwater it was more like a six-pack an evening, rather than one bottle or two. But he's never lost control with it, never seemed enslaved by it. Seeing him unscrew the bottle of rum I used to make my mojito last night and gulp the clear liquor straight from the bottle is both terrifying and tragic.

"Connor," I say softly. "I'm so sorry. About everything."

"Sorry." He doesn't look at me, just upturns the bottle into his mouth again. "Everyone is sorry tonight." He waves the bottle toward the open door, through which I can see Antoine leaning up against his truck, arms folded, his expression watchful. I can sense his reluctance to intervene and guess he doesn't want to make an awkward conversation worse. "Your husband," Connor says, putting a hard, sarcastic emphasis on the title, "has spent half the night apologizing for turning my beautiful girlfriend into a monster. Remy has spent two weeks being sorry that he can't seem to find a way to kill Keziah. Avery texts me every day saying how sorry she is for letting Keziah out of the cellar." He slams the refrigerator closed, hard enough that I jump. "You know who isn't sorry, Harper? You know who hasn't so much as met me face-to-face for the past two weeks?" He upturns the bottle again, watching me with hard, exhausted eyes. "Cass." His voice cracks on the name. "And everyone, from him"—he nods at Antoine—"to Remy, seems to be perfectly okay with that. They tell me not to try to find her, to leave it to them. Since I'm nothing more than just a powerless, weak human, who can, apparently, be killed in an instant, I'm supposed to simply sit here and wait for the monsters to sort it out amongst themselves. At least the wolves are actually trying to kill Keziah," he says bitterly. "Which is more than I can say for your husband. All he seems to care about is putting his damn hands all over you."

"That's enough!" I'm as shocked by his crudity as I am angry at the unfairness of what he's saying. "Did anyone tell you that the reason Antoine and Tate came for you tonight is because Keziah's threatened your life if you don't back off and leave Cass alone? That Cass herself told me to make you stay away from her—and did this to me, to prove her point?" I hold up my bandaged arm. The color drains from Connor's face. I don't feel any satisfaction knowing I've broken through his hard shell, just sadness that the only way of doing so is by causing yet more pain. "I know you want her back." I try to soften my tone. "So do I, Connor. I want Keziah dead just as much as you do."

"Then why aren't we doing something?" demands Connor. "At least Remy and the wolves are trying to track Keziah, to kill her."

"And how's that been going for them?" I fold my arms.

He shrugs and looks away. "At least they're trying," he mutters.

"Connor—Keziah is centuries old. Older than Antoine, or Tate. Even they don't know how old she is." I suppress a shudder as I remember Keziah's cold, venal eyes, the careless way she compelled one teacher, then casually fed from another. "Keziah has powers that nobody truly understands. She can't be killed like normal vampires. Burning doesn't harm her—or stakes, or sunlight. She rises from them all as if she's newly born. It's all been tried before. She isn't like others of her kind. Nobody really knows what she is.

"It isn't that Antoine doesn't want to kill her, Connor." I meet his eyes. "He just knows what doesn't work. And besides—Cass isn't the only one Keziah has power over." I glance sideways after I say this, in time to see Antoine's face tighten before he turns away.

Connor rubs a hand over the dark shadow on his jaw, his face lined with exhaustion. "All I know," he says bleakly, "is that every day Cass is under Keziah's control, I lose a little more of her. If we don't find a way to bring her back soon . . ." his voice trails off, and when he looks back at me, the stark desolation in his eyes makes my heart ache with sympathy. "I'm worried that if we don't bring her back soon, there will be nothing of the Cass we knew to bring back." He stares at me. "I can't give up on her, Harper. I won't. Not even if it means Keziah coming after me herself. I can't just let Cass disappear. If it means spending every night with the wolves, then that's what I'll do. But don't ask me to give up on her, Harper." His eyes search mine. "If it was Antoine," he says softly, "would you give up?"

When I don't answer, he nods. "That's what I thought." Handing me the open bottle of rum, he stumbles toward the staircase, bouncing off the walls as he goes.

I watch until he safely reaches the landing. I find the lid to the bottle, screw it on, and put it back on top of the refrigerator. The morning sun gleams off it as if to mock me, to remind me that the darkness is always waiting. I can feel Antoine watching me, waiting.

"I'll drive myself to school." My voice is unnaturally high. I run upstairs without looking at Antoine. I don't want him to see the tears I know I can't hide.

When I come back down half an hour later, however, he's still there, in the kitchen, a plate of pancakes on the table.

"I'm not hungry."

"You need to eat. Have you even slept? You shouldn't be at school today. You need to rest."

"What I need to do is get out of this house." I'm jittery and emotional. I feel like I've drunk a pint of coffee and followed it with whiskey chasers, my pulse racing and stomach churning. I can't think properly. I know it's probably lack of sleep as much as anything, but I don't feel even remotely tired. I can't face the thought of another encounter with Connor. Guilt and fear claw at my belly. I can't even bear to think of what life will look like if I lose my brother to the darkness.

"Harper." Antoine's eyes are dark with concern. "If you want to leave, that's fine. But I'm driving."

I'm too distracted to argue. The pancakes remain on the table, and we drive down the road, sun rising over the river haze, Spanish moss glistening on the live oak. Antoine drives with one large hand on the wheel, sprawled in the seat with casual grace, his long thighs hard and lean under the faded denim. I want to touch him so much it is like a physical pain. I don't know how to ask for what I want, and even if I did, I can't stand to be rejected again. It hurts more than my body. It hurts my soul.

I look out the window and fight the unwelcome tears hovering behind my eyes.

"It will get easier," Antoine says quietly. I swing around to face him, startled, worried he can read my mind. He's staring straight ahead, his jaw tense. "Connor. He'll get better. It just takes time, is all."

"Does it?" I lean back against the seat, not sure if I'm relieved or disappointed that it's Connor we are talking about. "Because he's right, you know. If it were you, I wouldn't give up. Not ever." His face tightens even more, and I go on, the turmoil inside making me reckless. "He wants to do something. He feels powerless, as if he's caught up in events he has no control over."

Antoine glances sideways at me. "Is it still Connor we're talking about?"

"It was you who worked the sun magic in Cass's body." I ignore his question. "You may not be her Maker, but you're connected to her by Keziah. You hear the same summons Cass does when Keziah calls you. Of everyone, you are the one person who has a chance of talking Cass around. Can you blame Connor for being angry that you won't try?" I know I'm goading him, but I can't help myself. I feel angry and frustrated, and not only on Connor's behalf.

Antoine's hands grip the steering wheel so tightly his knuckles are white. "Cass is different now. She's gone willingly to Keziah. She's killed for her, and with her. You don't know the power of those desires, Harper. The hunt, the kill—even alone they are potent. But Keziah's presence magnifies those urges, so they become all that exists. All that matters is obeying her voice, satisfying the urges she rouses."

I think bitterly that I know all about desire right now. I wonder if he even sees the irony in what he's saying. "It's like a gnawing hunger that can never be quite satiated," he goes on, his voice hard and tight. "Her approval is a drug you can never quite get enough of. It twists inside, turns you half mad with the desire to please her. It's as if the only way you can ever know satisfaction is in satiating Keziah's desires, but those desires themselves are insatiable, the depths of her darkness unfathomable." He glances at me, his eyes dark and cavernous. "I can't pull Cass back from that, Harper. Nobody can. The only thing that can pull Cass back is Cass herself, and until and unless she decides to do so, she is more dangerous than you can begin to imagine."

He turns back to stare through the windshield, and I can no longer read his eyes. "I know Connor wants to bring her back," he says after a moment, his voice a little calmer. "I understand how he feels. But if you believe anything, Harper, please believe this: there is nothing that you or Connor can do that will change what is happening inside Cass. The only thing you can do is let it play out—and stay safe while it does."

His efforts to restrain his every emotion serve only to fuel to my own. Every word he says exacerbates my feelings of impotence and frustration.

"Stay safe?" The tension inside twists and turns, becoming fractious anger. "None of us are safe, Antoine. Not you, not Tate, not Remy and his wolves. And most of all, not my brother. There isn't anything I can say that will make him give up on helping Cass. And honestly, despite everything you just said, I can't believe you're willing to give up on her either. It isn't right, Antoine. You can't keep everyone safe from everything. Sometimes you just have to let go, and trust that it will turn out, somehow."

Frustration causes tears to lurk behind my eyes again and I turn to the window, blinking blindly against the white sunlight.

Antoine pulls into the school lot and parks, turning to me. "Is it still Cass we're talking about?"

"There is so much you won't share with me." I can't look at him. "Please don't tell me I'm imagining things, or that it's for my own safety. You give me half-truths, snippets of information. But for some reason you don't trust me enough to truly talk to me. I can feel it, all that you're holding back. You don't even trust me enough to be—properly married to me," I finish lamely.

I open the door and leap out of the truck before he can ask what I mean, but he's faster, and I find myself trapped in the door of the truck, his hands on the roof on either side of my head, his tall, bronzed body so close to mine I can barely breathe, the storm-tossed eyes boring into my own. "You think it's because I don't trust you that I won't allow myself to lose control?" He speaks in a low voice that sends a shiver down my spine and turns my body to liquid. The thumb of his right hand grazes my cheekbone, trails down my neck so my breath catches.

"I don't understand why you don't—you won't—" my voice trails off and fiery color blazes over my face.

And then he is kissing me so fiercely all I know is blinding light behind my closed lids, and desire so savage I forget everything but the heat of his mouth and hands.

"Miss Ellory!" Somewhere through a dim haze I hear my old name being called. "Miss Ellory!"

Antoine moves his mouth from mine. His lips brush my ear. "They're calling you."

Reluctantly I open my eyes and turn slightly, to find Mr. Larkin standing, red-faced and indignant, by his car. "I thought Tate compelled him to leave," I mutter in a shaky voice. I feel the rumble of Antoine's laughter. He still hasn't moved, and I become uncomfortably aware that my leg is around his waist, one of his hands holding it up, his fingers hot and strong through my jeans. "Not leave." Antoine makes no attempt at all to move. "Mr. Larkin is busy doing lesson planning. He will be for the rest of the term, while the new teacher gives him a much-needed break." Turning to look at Mr. Larkin, he raises one hand in a slightly sarcastic wave, then, quite pointedly, kisses me again.

"Have a good day," he murmurs against my cheek. "Play nice with others." Turning his head, he grins at Mr. Larkin. "And you," he says, for the second day in a row, smiling lazily. "You have a good day, now."

Sauntering around the truck, he gets in, waiting until I scurry past Mr. Larkin's lowered brows before he drives away, leaving me breathless and disheveled as I climb the steps to school, trying to make sense of what just happened.

CHAPTER 7

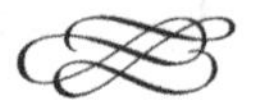

GARRISON

Perhaps it's the skin memory of Antoine's body against mine. Perhaps it's anger at seeing my brother so heartbroken. Or maybe I'm simply so tired of feeling afraid that there's no more fear left inside me. But when I walk into history class to find Keziah flanked by Cass and Caleb, twirling a pencil through her long curls as she smiles insolently at me, I don't feel at all intimidated. I meet Keziah's eyes and hold them, then take my seat, as if there is nothing at all odd about having three vampires barely yards away. I feel both pity and anger when I look at Cass. I wish she weren't going through this. But I wish even more that I didn't have to watch my brother suffer while Cass decides whether or not he is worth fighting her Maker's desires for.

"Harper." Avery leans across the aisle toward me. "Your sweater is on inside out." I glance down and feel my face flame yet again. I don't remember the knit sweater coming off in the parking lot, nor putting it back on.

I seem to remember very little, after Antoine starts kissing me.

Avery smirks as I whip my sweater off and put it back on,

the right way around this time. I look up to find Keziah watching me through narrowed eyes. She isn't smiling anymore. I find that immensely satisfying.

I sit up straighter in my chair and try to focus on Tate's lesson. A moment later my attention is gone again, derailed by the silent vibration of my phone. Avery has sent me a text: *Spent last night with Remy and wolves. Healers in his family teaching me a lot.*

Good? I answer, unsure how to respond to this. It seems everyone is hanging out with wolves. Avery is learning to use her Natchez blood; Connor is spending his nights roaming the bayous with Remy, trying to fight back against Keziah. While I, I think, punching my pen savagely into my page, just dig in my night garden and try to seduce my husband.

I feel the familiar wave of despondency approach.

"I know you've covered some of the French wars in the early eighteenth century," Tate is saying up the front of the class, "but I'd like to focus a little on the Natchez culture that existed here before the settlers came." He heads off into a discussion about the unique social structure maintained by the Natchez, including matrilineal kinship, which he explains means that descent was determined along female rather than male lines. He also says that unlike many Native American tribes, among certain tribes of Natchez the practice of marrying outside of the tribe was common—encouraged, even. For once the entire class is listening and asking questions. Somehow he makes the world of the early Natchez come to life, describing the Tattooed Serpent and the Great Sun in such vivid detail it's like we are all seeing it as it once was. It's mind-bending for me to remember that Tate actually lived through those days, is himself a descendant of the Great Sun, and was once designated to be the next Tattooed Serpent. I try and fail to imagine how it must have been to watch the destruction of his world, to live long enough to see an entire way of life disappear, his own stories forgotten.

I'm lost in his words when Keziah interrupts Tate.

"Mr. Garrison." I'm faintly shocked to realize I've never before heard Tate's last name said aloud. "What do you know about the attack on the French garrison during those years, the one where dozens of French soldiers were found dead?" She looks around at the class. "Oh!" she says, feigning surprise. "I never thought about it, but your surname is Garrison, just like the French garrison that was attacked! What a coincidence."

She sits back in her chair, spinning her pencil on its point, a small smile on her face. But if she hopes to discomfort Tate, she is disappointed. The expression of polite interest on his face never wavers.

"Miss Joseph makes an excellent point," Tate says easily. "There were several attacks on local garrisons during the era. Some were brutal indeed. Bodies were found with throats torn out, sometimes entirely drained of blood. There were many stories of what creatures might cause such chaos and destruction. Some blamed animals, though most, of course, blamed either slaves or the Natchez." He meets Keziah's eyes steadily. "Survivors of one particularly gruesome attack claimed the entire event had been the work of one woman. A beautiful slave. A demon who could control the minds of men." I can barely breathe. I wonder that the tension seems to go largely unnoticed by the class, but then, I think rather disjointedly, none of them could possibly suspect that the demon Tate is talking about is sitting right in the room with them at this moment.

"Of course," Tate smiles around at the class, "Nobody now would believe such a story. But those were dark days, and people were more superstitious then." His eyes swivel back to Keziah. "Despite not entirely believing the account, the French nonetheless carried out vicious acts of reprisal against local slaves. Many hundreds of them died. Terrible, agonizing deaths." He holds her eyes. "Even though there was no evidence at all that the slaves had anything to do with the attacks on the French forces."

Keziah's smile has disappeared. She waits a beat after he's finished, then comes right back at him.

"I was thinking more about one attack in particular." Her voice is hard and pointed. "I read about it at the historical society. Survivors of that attack also claimed it was the work of one person. A deranged, bloodthirsty Natchez savage who slaughtered everyone in his path."

"'Savage' is not a term we use in this classroom," says Tate quietly. "And yes, that attack was one of the darker episodes of local history. By all accounts it was indeed the work of one man. He must have been truly depraved—mad, even, to cause the willful death of so many."

Given that I know the man in question was Tate himself, I'm astonished at his restraint. *And to take the name Garrison,* I think. Branding himself for life with a reminder of his own crimes.

"It's a pity he was never caught," murmurs Keziah.

"Oh," says Tate lightly, "After such terrible crimes, I suspect his conscience would have been all the punishment he ever needed." They are staring at each other, and I can almost feel Keziah using every ounce of her mind control to attempt to manipulate Tate, to humiliate him as she did Mr. Larkin. Tate, however, is resisting her, though I can see by his tense stance and clenched jaw that it is taking a deal of effort to do so. I hadn't realized she had this much influence over even unrelated vampires, though I suppose that strictly speaking Tate isn't unrelated, if he was made by Antoine.

One of the other students asks a question and the tension is broken, though I can tell Keziah is not satisfied. She's looking around the classroom, seeking another outlet for her anger. Her eyes rest on the bandage covering the cut on my arm. I pull my sleeve down and try to ignore her.

After what seems an interminable time, the bell goes. In the clatter of chairs and books, I find Keziah standing in front of me. She seizes my arm, her grip so strong it's impossible for me to pull away, and turns it over, pulling the sleeve up and bandage off to show the livid red line beneath it. Cass and Caleb hover a short distance away, their eyes gleaming with predatory excitement. "Antoine didn't heal you with his blood." It's a statement, not a question.

Tate appears at my side. The classroom is empty of normal students, leaving just Jeremiah and Avery beside us, eyeing the vampires warily.

"Let her go, Keziah," says Tate quietly. "There is no gain for you in hurting Harper."

Keziah goes on as if he hasn't spoken. "Antoine wouldn't allow Takatoka to give you his blood, either, would he?" She shoots Tate a scathing glance. "I do beg your pardon. *Tate,* as he calls himself these days. Tate Garrison. Are you so proud of your handiwork you wished to be known by it for the rest of eternity, Takatoka?" She shakes her head in mock remonstration, still holding my arm. "You and Antoine. Forever obsessed by moral right. You could both have been so much more. And now look at you." She drops my arm disdainfully and steps back. "Still dallying with humans, and still afraid to grasp power when it is so closely within reach."

Her eyes narrow as she looks me up and down. "He hasn't lain with you." Again it's a statement rather than a question.

"Keziah . . ."

"We were lovers, you know." Ignoring Tate, Keziah addresses me. "Antoine and I. There was a time when he desired me so much he would do anything—anything at all—that I asked of him." Her topaz eyes gleam with malevolence. "Your historical records document some of his finer moments." Her tone is low, sibilant. "There was no savagery from which Antoine shied, no deed too dark or terrible he would not do it. All because he wanted me." One hand touches my face, and it takes all my willpower not to step away. "But now he will not lie with you." Her words slice my heart with surgical precision. "Antoine is not a man who should be without a woman. I wonder what it can be, that holds him back from giving you his blood—or lying with you?" I have an uncharacteristic urge to slap the knowing, sneering smile off her face. "Hm." Her lips tilt in a mocking smile. "And that mind of yours, that cannot be compelled. What mysteries lie there, yet to be uncovered? I wonder how much Antoine truly knows about you. I wonder what he will tell you of himself—and what he will continue to hide." Her gloating eyes linger long enough to make it clear she knows exactly how furious and frustrated her words make me feel. Then she turns to Tate, her face hardening.

"I shall enjoy our history classes together, Mr. Garrison. I feel there is so much I've missed during my slumber. And yet there are things I remember. Things in the soil I can feel still." The topaz eyes gleam. "Marguerite Marigny, for instance," she says silkily. "Her body I sense in the earth. I visit with her sometimes, Takatoka. She cannot hide behind that name anymore. Not in death."

Tate lunges forward, snarling savagely, but Keziah is already gone, her mocking laughter echoing down the corridor. I stand frozen in place, Keziah's words echoing through my heart, watching Tate's rigid back in silent sympathy, knowing there is nothing I can possibly say that will help.

CHAPTER 8

LORE

I lurch uneasily through the day, jittery with lack of sleep and nerves. Tate left quickly after his encounter with Keziah. I know he's uncomfortable that he lost control like that. I understand it entirely, however. I had a few moments where I could have torn Keziah's eyes out myself, even if I knew that doing so would mean my own end. I figure it would be almost worth it to see that sneering, sadistic smile wiped from her exquisitely perfect face. Of all the things I should be concerned about, Keziah's taunts regarding the intimate nature of her relationship with Antoine back in the day should be at the bottom of the list. Instead they're right there at the top, front and center, making it hard for me to so much as think about anything else.

"Pardon?" I realize Avery is talking to me during art that afternoon. I'm trying to paint the night garden, but my hands tremble, and I can't seem to focus.

"I said, what did Keziah mean, about visiting with Marguerite Marigny?" Avery shoots me a sideways look. "Jeremiah told me that Marguerite was Antoine's sister. She must have died centuries ago. Why was Tate so upset when her name was mentioned?"

I wash my paintbrush as I weigh honesty against Tate's trust. Then I figure that most of what I know is more or less public record for the Natchez.

"Tate loved her." Quickly I fill Avery in on the history: Tate's love for Marguerite, his intention to marry her, and Antoine's sacrifice—becoming a vampire made with Natchez blood to save them all from Keziah's reign of terror. "But Antoine was almost mad by the time he conquered Keziah's voice in his mind," I say. "He turned Tate during that time, destroying any chance Tate had of happiness with Marguerite. Tate compelled Marguerite to forget him. It was only at the end of her life, after her human husband was gone, that he returned to comfort her in her final years. I don't think he's ever really gotten over her." Now that I say it aloud, I know it's true. Tate, I suspect, has never truly allowed himself to love again since Marguerite. Part of that—maybe more than part—is tied to his relationship to Antoine, the guilt he carries even now over what Antoine did to save his sister. I know that Antoine would have made the same choice with or without Tate, but something tells me Tate will never believe that. "For Tate to imagine that Keziah is somehow torturing Marguerite's spirit beyond the grave, beyond any dimension in which Tate could help, must be unbearable," I finish.

Avery is pale, her paintbrush forgotten. "What a story." She stares into the distance, as if seeing the tragedy in her mind. "What is Keziah, then? If she has all these other powers—to reach beyond death, to survive when she should be burned to dust—if Keziah isn't a vampire, what is she?"

I shrug. "I don't know. Nor, it seems, does anyone else."

"She seemed very interested in you." Avery looks at me curiously. "What did she mean, about your mind? Is she right, that you can't be compelled?"

"I'm sure there are other people out there who can't be compelled." I look away from her.

"Maybe," Avery says doubtfully. "But it must be very rare. I can't find anything about it in all the stuff I've read."

"You've been reading?" I seize on the change of subject. "Is there some kind of handbook for Natchez magic?"

"Not exactly." But the gleam in Avery's eye tells me my feeble attempt at humor isn't too far from the truth. "Remy's mother, Lori, works at the historical center. She's an elder of their tribe and goes to Oklahoma regularly to meet with other descendants of the Natchez nation. She's also skilled in herb lore and the stories of our people. She's been helping me understand what I am—what I can do."

"And what are you?" I'm beginning to wonder if anyone in Deepwater Hollow is really what they seem—normal teenagers, going to high school.

"Well, I knew I was descended from the family of the original Great Sun. Noya said as much when she was here." I nod. I remember. "So it seems that the last of my line to live in the old way was a woman they called the White Sun: a noble, the eldest of the Sun women. She was known for her ability to channel spirits and bid them do her will. Lori believes that I may have inherited some of that ability, and that's why Keziah found it so easy to get into my mind. She's helping me learn how to block spirits I don't want, to find the ones I do, and channel their power."

"Wow." I stare at her. "You mean, like a witch?"

"Not exactly. I don't really know what I am, yet." The gleam in her eye fades. "But if I can channel something that might help Cass," she says soberly, "it seems like I should do all I can to find out."

I turn her words over in my mind during the afternoon. I'm still not tired, though I feel spaced out from the lack of sleep.

My nerves are hardening into resolve after my discussion with Avery.

In all that has happened since I met Antoine, I've barely had time to think about the fact that I can't be compelled. It seemed to get thrust to the back of my mind, along with all the other things I haven't had time to consider. But now I mull over Keziah's words, trying to make sense of them. The more that I ponder them, the more I think of what Avery said, about finding out what she is in case there is a way to help Cass.

What if I am something, too? What if Keziah isn't just playing with me—what if she means that I have some kind of power? And what if that power could actually help free Cass—and stop my brother from putting his life in danger?

The more I think about it, the more determined I become to find out what it is that Antoine isn't telling me. By the time school is done, I'm searching the parking lot eagerly. Antoine is already there, leaning against the truck, eyes narrowed as he watches Keziah, Caleb, and Cass glide across the playing field, surrounded by a group of admirers, including Jared Baudelaire, who is staring at Cass with puppy-doglike admiration. I grit my teeth. I know Cass and the other two have been feeding off high school students; I've never seen so many neck scarves. I can only hope they stop at feeding.

Antoine waits until we pull out of the lot. "Well?"

"Well what?"

"I know that look." He shoots me a wry smile. "You may as well ask whatever it is you want to know and get it over with."

"Okay, then." I take a deep breath. "Keziah told me about the two of you. That you used to be . . . together."

"Together," he says flatly.

"Lovers." I hate that word, but I don't know how else to say it without sounding coarse.

"Love had nothing to do with what Keziah and I were." The

humorous edge has left his voice. He looks straight ahead and drives a little too fast.

"But she was right," I say. "You were with her, after you were first turned."

"That is technically correct. Yes."

"Keziah knew that you and I—that we haven't been together, like that. She mentioned it." When he doesn't speak, I glance over at him. "How would she know something like that? Can she read your mind? Or compel you to tell her?"

It's a while before he answers. The winter sky is thin and orange with the fading day, and the river smells dank and cold, the rich scent of summer far away. It feels hard, I think absent-mindedly. The air feels hard.

"What else did Keziah say?" His tone is carefully neutral, giving nothing away, and I feel suddenly certain there is a great deal here that I don't understand.

"She knew you hadn't given me your blood when I was wounded by Cass. She made a point of questioning why that was."

"I've already told you—"

"I know what you told me, Antoine." I twist in my seat so I can watch him. "I just don't believe you." When he doesn't answer, I go on: "Keziah commented on the fact that I can't be compelled. It made me realize that you've never said why that is, or even so much as discussed it. And she said something else. At the time it kind of passed me by, but later I thought about it, and realized how strange it was." When he doesn't answer, I continue. "She said that you and Tate are both afraid to grasp power when it is so closely within reach." I wait for a beat. "I think the power she was talking about has something to do with me. I want to know what she meant. Especially if whatever it is might somehow be able to help Cass."

Antoine turns into the driveway, shadows flickering inside

the car as we drive under the long tunnel of live oak toward the mansion. Connor's truck is gone, and there is nobody else here but us. Antoine pulls up. Neither of us get out.

"I've told you before that Keziah is manipulative and dangerous." His voice is steady, but I can hear the tension behind his words, and he doesn't meet my eyes. "She will do everything she can to unsettle you, to sow doubt in your mind—in all of our minds. She's more dangerous than anything you can imagine. Nothing she says can be trusted. And if you try to interfere in her bond with Cass, there's no limit to what she will do to stop you." He gets out of the truck and is at my side with the door open in a moment. "You have to promise me you won't get between Keziah and Cass, Harper."

I step out of the truck. "I'm getting a little tired of promises like that. Especially when I know you aren't telling me the truth."

"I'm telling you everything you need to know."

"And I take it you're the one who decides what I need to know." I'm tired. No, actually, I'm exhausted. I'm also angry. I face him over the hood. "I married you because I wanted to protect my brother, the person I love, by putting my name on the title to the house and keeping the binding intact. All I've ever wanted to do is keep the people I love safe. But they aren't safe anymore, Antoine. And if being married means you controlling everything, from where I go, to the information I have, then maybe you're right not to make ours a 'real' marriage. It's starting to feel to me like it might have been built on lies from the start."

We stare at each other for a long moment, but when he doesn't say anything, I eventually turn away. When I close the kitchen door behind me, part of me hopes he might follow.

But he doesn't, and a short time later, I hear the truck start up and drive away.

Too drained to make any sense of it all, I throw myself face-down on my bed, and fall instantly into a deep sleep.

I WAKE SOMEWHERE PAST MIDNIGHT. THE MOON IS LONG GONE, the night cold and still. I pad downstairs and to my surprise, find not Connor or Antoine, but Tate sitting at the kitchen table, staring into the darkness, a glass of neat whiskey in front of him. He jolts slightly as I come in, his voice husky when he speaks.

"Antoine asked me to stay here tonight. He was worried about you being alone."

"Antoine specializes in worrying." My voice sounds cracked and tired. "Perhaps he should try telling the truth a little more and worrying about me a little less." A few hours sleep has done nothing to alleviate my anger at Antoine's refusal to tell me the truth, simply dulled it to a hurtful ache.

"The truth isn't always helpful." Tate speaks without moving at all, staring out the window down toward the river. It takes a moment for me to realize where he is looking—in the direction of the tree beneath which Marguerite is buried.

"What Keziah said today," I say. "About contacting Marguerite. Did you believe her?"

"Yes."

It's such a simple, heartbreaking answer that I'm temporarily shocked into silence. For a while neither of us say anything.

"I've spent the past three centuries trying to understand what Keziah is." Tate's voice is quiet in the darkness. "My search has taken me all over the world, from South America to the Caribbean, from Africa to Australia. I've researched every type of world mythology, legends from across the globe. Antoine was never so dedicated. I think it was too close, the threat of Keziah's return too horrifying. Nor could he see her separately from his experience of her, if that makes sense. I think Antoine just wanted to forget Keziah, and the person he was when he was with her." He glances at me. "I told you once he was almost mad when he overcame their bond. That kind of experience changes a person, Harper. The thought of being controlled like that again—or worse, of seeing you under her control —is too much, I think, for Antoine to even begin to contemplate."

I'm not in the mood, though, to hear excuses for Antoine. "After all that time researching, do you know what Keziah is?"

"I have some ideas. But nothing certain." Seeing the look on my face, he nods. "I can tell you some of what I believe. Keziah's powers are linked to earth magic. That is a very different quality in a vampire, for we are a biological mutation, more separate from the organic world than possibly any other being in existence. Vampires such as Antoine, myself, and Cass, with our sun totems, are a rarity. I know of only a few others with anything similar. It makes us unique, something Keziah recognized right from the start. I believe that is why she coveted Antoine so very badly after he was made. Not only because she wanted him, as she had wanted many human playthings, but because he possessed sun magic, which fascinated her. She, too, has powers of regeneration that I believe are linked to earth magic. Magic I still don't understand, and not of this place, or at least not that I recognise. She and Caleb wear talismans, so I don't believe she possesses it in her body, as we do."

"But you think she can contact those buried in the earth?"

"The mystery of what happens after we die is one none of us know, even those of us who are dead. I'm not convinced it is the actual physical presence that triggers her communication. But I think that when people die, they leave a shadow of themselves, a presence, in certain places. Places where they left part of their soul, where they became part of the earth and wind." I try not to show how jolted I am by his words. "Marguerite spent every day of her life on this land. She loved it, despite everything. Sometimes I think I hear her, in the whisper of wind, the call of birds. Smell her in the magnolias she loved so much." It's so close to how I feel about Tessa that his words make me feel both closer to Tate and even lonelier, if possible, than I did before. What if my imaginings are no more than the same fantasies everyone has about those they've lost? Does everyone imagine they hear echoes on the wind—and if so, are we lying to ourselves, or truly hearing what we think we do?

"So, yes, Harper," Tate continues. "I think Keziah can speak to that part of Marguerite, the part left in the earth here." He turns to me. "But do I believe she can torture Marguerite, across the dimension of death? No. That, I believe, is part of Keziah's devilment, no more than a spur she uses to goad me. Marguerite died in peace, her heart content and her life fulfilled. She died in love with me, if I dare say so. There is no part of her that lingers in anger, to be used against us. I don't believe that. I can't."

We sit in silence for a time. He pours me a glass of whiskey and I sip it neat, savoring the fiery rush despite having never particularly liked it before.

"I know you want to understand what Keziah meant, when she talked about you today." Tate glances at me. "Antoine didn't tell me you had asked him, but I gathered as much from his dark mood and his request for me to stay here tonight." He pours more whiskey into my glass. "I will tell you only what I know to be true." His smile has a grim edge. "Not what might be."

I nod. Anything, I think, is better than knowing nothing.

Tate rolls the glass meditatively between his hands. "In all I have learned of supernatural creatures, there are only a few who are impervious to compulsion. And all of them are connected to earth magic."

"Earth magic." I repeat the words slowly. "What do you mean by that?"

"There are many types of creatures that are connected to the earth. I'm not going to speculate too much." His eyes flick up to me then back to his glass. "But I had my first suspicions about you when the red magnolia trees here kept blooming, after the summer was over. New ones grew, also, in places I've never known them to be, as if they simply appeared overnight."

"I've always been able to grow things." I hear the defensive note in my voice. "Mom was the same. And Tessa had plants, even in the hospital."

"Exactly." Tate nods as if this is evidence of his point, rather than a refutation. "It would have run in your family. It's likely always been the women, too—men rarely possess the same connection. Then there was your imperviousness to compulsion," he continues. "And your blood—I couldn't understand why it was that Keziah didn't attack you as soon as she escaped. You'd thwarted her plans not once, but twice, ensuring she remained locked in that cellar. She had every reason to destroy you. And yet she didn't so much as touch you. But it was when you planted the night garden that your true abilities became undeniable."

Tate looks down the hill into the darkness, where the night garden will even now be opening under the moon. "Most of those plants barely survive this close to the river. Water lilies aren't known for loving this part of the Mississippi. And none of them flourish in the dead of winter." He meets my eyes. "It's been less than a month since you planted that garden, Harper. Yet the plants in it are already high as my knee, colors and species I've never seen grow here before. Moonvine clings to your window frame; in three centuries, it's never flourished in this garden."

"What are you saying?" I'm confused. "That I'm some kind of . . . spirit?"

"All I know," he says soberly, "is that whatever you are is linked to the earth. Any such power is significant, no matter how latent it may be within you. Keziah can feel it—and she is fascinated by it." In the shadows of the night his eyes are dark and serious. "That's what terrifies Antoine, Harper. It isn't that he is trying to hide anything from you. He's terrified that Keziah knows the truth of whatever that power is—and that she's using Cass as bait to harness it."

CHAPTER 9

MAGIC

We talk for a little longer, but it's clear that Tate has said either as much as he knows or is willing to tell me. Either way, the most I can wring from him is that I'm not a witch, or a medicine woman, or even a herbalist. In fact, I can't see a single benefit in my magical green thumb other than that I seem able to grow unusual plants.

Not exactly an earth-shattering power. Not immortality, or preternatural speed. Not natural psychic ability like Avery, or whatever it is that makes Remy and his clan turn into wolves. Nothing that can help Cass. Only some odd power I don't even understand, and that for some reason, Keziah covets. Which means my mere existence is putting people in danger—again.

I slip out of the back door and down to my night garden, feeling almost guilty that I'm seeking solace in the earth. It might be living evidence of whatever powers I have, but the night garden is also my greatest source of comfort, and the place where I feel closest to Tessa. "Whatever we are didn't help you, in the end, did it?" I whisper as I put my fingers in the soil, wishing, for a sudden, savage moment of breathless heartache, that my beautiful sister could somehow answer me. "All the earth magic in the world couldn't heal your kidneys. It made no difference to Mom's cancer. What point is there in having some weird ability to make plants grow?" Tears roll off my face and fall into the warm, scented river soil. I carry on, muttering away to Tessa, wiping dirt across my face when I dash away the tears.

"You know they say that talking to yourself is the first sign of madness."

I swing around, startled, and find Connor smiling crookedly at me in the gloom. I'm so happy to see him both sober and smiling that I throw my arms around his neck and for a moment we just stand there, in a wordless hug that says more than explanations ever could. Eventually he pats my back and I let go, grateful the night dark and dirt on my face disguise my emotions.

"I'm glad you're gardening again." He nods at the pale flowers open beneath the growing moon. "It reminds me of Tessa and Mom."

"I put the last of Tessa's ashes here." I glance at him. "I hope that's okay."

"It's perfect." Connor sits on the ground beside the garden, his hands hanging loosely over his knees. "She always loved magnolia trees, and this place is surrounded by them." He looks over at the edge of the lawn. "They must be different to the trees we had in Louisiana. Those never flowered in the winter."

I stab the fork into the earth, then lift it with enough violence to spray dirt several feet.

"Hey," Connor says. "I thought it was me doing anger management this week."

"Well." I stab the earth again. "I guess it must be therapy week at the Marigny Mansion."

"Want to talk about it?"

"Not really." I make a concerted effort to dig less vigorously. "I'm glad you're doing better, Connor."

"I'm not, really." His voice sounds tired. "But I'm not a wolf, and I'm not a vampire, and as your husband pointed out rather forcefully to me tonight, the fact that I'm neither of those things means I'm basically useless." For once, there's no edge to his voice when he says the word husband. Unfortunately, it's also the first time I've found it annoying rather than thrilling to hear the word said aloud.

"Oh?" I try to keep my voice neutral. "And what exactly did Antoine decide to 'point out' to you?"

"He didn't compel me, if that's what you're asking. Although he did mention that if I didn't come home straight away and talk to you, that he'd wait until every ounce of frankincense was out of my system, and then compel me to do so." Connor gives me a wry grin. "At least he gave me the choice."

"I thought Antoine would be the last person you'd listen to."

"He didn't really give me the option to walk away. But maybe I needed to hear some of what he said." Connor glances sideways at me, then away again. "I didn't think of what would happen if Keziah forced Cass to kill me, or you. Cass could never forgive herself for that. Antoine said that if she crosses that line, does something that makes her believe she is beyond redemption, it would make it that much harder for Cass to ever be who she was before. He said that Keziah won't hesitate to make Cass do something like that—kill one of us, or Cass's mother, even. And I guess Antoine knows Keziah better than anyone else."

"Oh, he certainly does." I stab the ground again.

"Harper?" Connor leans forward. "What's going on?"

"It doesn't matter." I sit back and rest my elbows on my knees, the fork dangling between them.

"Is it about Antoine? Because although I might not like the fact that you're married to him—okay, I don't like it at all—even I can see that he's in love with you. And I do believe he'll do everything in his power to protect you."

"Except for telling me the truth."

"The truth about what?"

I thrust the fork viciously into the soil, where it sticks, the handle quivering. The last thing Connor needs is more to worry about. "It's nothing." I keep my voice calm with an effort. "Truly. Just a private disagreement. I shouldn't have mentioned it."

"Harper." Connor's eyes slide over my face. "Look where secrets have led to. If there's something I should know, then tell me. I don't blame you for what happened to Cass. But I think I've earned the right to honesty."

I lean back and meet his eyes. "You're right," I say quietly. "I never should have lied to you. And I'm more sorry than I can ever say for what has happened to Cass. I guess I just don't want to add to your troubles, and I know that talking about this with you will do that."

Connor laughs without humor. "It gets to a point where there are so many troubles, I guess another one can't really hurt."

"This one might, though." I take a deep breath. "Did you know I can't be compelled?"

Connor looks surprised. "No, I didn't. But that must be a good thing, isn't it?" He smiles despite himself. "If you're going to be married to a vampire, I mean. I can see how compulsion might cause an issue or too." He tilts his head, turning his mouth down at the corners. "Oddly, that actually makes me feel better about you and Antoine."

"It won't when I tell you why." I gesture at the garden. "Have you ever wondered why I can make a garden anywhere—even in that horrible little apartment we had in Baton Rouge years ago, where it was all concrete and darkness?"

Connor's mouth tilts at the edges. "All three of you could grow plants anywhere. It was one of the things I always loved about being with you." I look at him in surprise; I'd never known that. Strange, I think, how little we sometimes know about those closest to us. Connor has always praised my painting, but I don't ever remember him talking about my potted plants or little kitchen gardens.

"Well, as it turns out, apparently there is something supernatural about my ability to grow things."

It feels strange saying it aloud.

"Supernatural?" Connor frowns. "How?"

"I don't know, exactly." I shrug. "I only found out today, and only then because of something Keziah said. Whatever power I have, it seems Keziah not only knows about it, but also has plans to harness it. Tate says that's why Antoine is so worried about Keziah getting close to me. He doesn't want her to gain access to whatever I am."

"And Antoine didn't tell you any of this," says Connor flatly.

"No. I only know as much as I do because Tate told me."

"So Tate knows what you are. Antoine knows what you are." I can hear the anger building in his voice. "In fact, it's quite possible that one of the reasons Keziah took Cass in the first place is because she, too, knows what you are, and wanted leverage to use against you."

I nod unhappily. "It's my fault, Connor. All of it."

"No, it isn't." Connor stands up abruptly. "There's only one person responsible for this. For all of this. And I'm going to damn well make Antoine tell us both everything he knows about whatever this power is. Whatever it is that you are."

There's something ugly about the way he says the last words that hurts me, deep inside. "You say that as if I'm some sort of freak." I look at him. "You told me you wanted the truth, Connor. This is the truth."

"That my sister is what—some sort of witch?" His voice is rising, and I can feel that I'm losing him. I spring to my feet, but a voice behind me interrupts smoothly before I can say anything.

"She isn't a witch, Connor. She's a nature spirit—or the descendant of one."

We both swing around as Antoine steps from the shadows. His face is grave, and he's looking at Connor, not me.

"A nature spirit?" Connor stares at him. "I don't even understand what that means."

Antoine comes closer.

"Legend has it that every plant and tree has an earth spirit, a personality of sorts. An essence." He's still talking to Connor, not me.

"The spirits once took human form, as well as plant form. They're known in mythology by different names—dryads, nymphs. But they aren't witches." Antoine's eyes shift to me. "They don't create magic," he says quietly. "Nature spirits are magic. They hold the power of the earth in their bodies. That's why you can't be compelled, Harper."

"And you just decided to tell us this now," says Connor, his voice low and furious. "You didn't think to tell Harper about this, oh, I don't know—before you married her?"

"I didn't know then." Antoine's eyes flicker to where Tate's figure is emerging from the darkness several feet from us. "I'm still not entirely certain, which is why I hadn't planned to say anything at all, at least until I'd had a chance to learn more. The fewer people who know what Harper might be, the safer we all are. Unfortunately"—he glares at Tate—"I wasn't given a choice in the matter."

"She has a right to know, brother," says Tate quietly.

"None of us knows anything," Antoine snaps back.

"Is anyone even going to ask what I think about all this?" I look between the three of them, Connor red-faced and angry, Antoine grim and dark, Tate quietly apologetic. "You're all busy deciding what is best for me, but not one of you has asked what I think about this. About being some kind of —fairy."

"You're not a—"

"I don't care what you call it!" I round on Tate so furiously that he subsides immediately. "I don't understand any of this. But why is it that I still feel there is more I don't know?"

"More you don't know?" Connor snorts. "At least you can't be compelled to forget what you do know." He glares at Antoine. "Only an hour ago, you stood in front of me and told me that I was putting Cass in danger by trying to seek her out. That Keziah wouldn't hesitate to kill me or Harper to keep Cass at her side. But that was just more lies, wasn't it? What you really meant was that you wanted to keep Harper to yourself. Your own personal magical creature. One who just might have power that you can harness for your own strength."

"Connor—" I put a hand on his arm, but Connor shakes it off angrily.

"No, Harper. Ever since the start of this entire nightmare, one question has been bothering me: why would a three-century-old vampire, a man who's seen the world and everything in it, suddenly fall in love with a seventeen-year-old girl? But all this time, it wasn't Harper you were in love with, was it, Antoine?" He shakes his head, mouth twisted in disgust. "It's always been about *what* Harper is, not who."

With lethal, preternatural swiftness Antoine's hand is around his neck and Connor is hard up against a tree, his feet dangling above the ground. "You know nothing," Antoine growls. "Nothing at all."

"Don't I," gasps Connor, staring straight at Antoine without the slightest hint of remorse. Just as quickly, Tate is there, murmuring something to Antoine, who lowers Connor slowly to the ground, though his eyes are still gleaming with gold fury. Connor hits away Antoine's hand, and turns to me. "Well?" he says coldly. "Are you going to stay with him, knowing this?"

"I don't—I have to talk—" I'm stuttering, unable to find the words. "Please don't go," I say lamely. "You've only just come back."

"I came back to lies." Connor regards the three of us with

palpable disgust. "I won't stay and listen to any more of them. I'm done, Harper. I'm done with all of you."

Turning, he strides up the hill, until the darkness swallows him. A few moments later I hear the sound of his truck start up. He roars down the driveway and is gone.

Something tells me that this time, he won't be coming back.

CHAPTER 10

OUTSIDER

"Harper." Antoine puts a hand on my shoulder. I whirl to face him, and whatever he sees in my face is enough to make him take a step backward. He shakes his head. "I didn't want to tell you half a story," he says. "What I said to Connor is the truth. Most of what I know is only suspicion and speculation. It may be nothing at all."

"Except that I can't be compelled." I stare at him. "And I'm guessing that's more than a little rare, Antoine. I would bet this entire mansion that in three centuries, neither of you has ever met anyone else who couldn't be compelled."

Neither Tate nor Antoine correct me.

"Which means I'm *something*." My voice is slightly unsteady. "Some kind of—supernatural creature. Earth spirit." I stare at the night garden, then back at Antoine. The dawn is growing, and his eyes gleam, gold on cobalt. "Was Connor right?" The words hurt my throat. I'm aware of Tate moving quietly away, heading diplomatically back toward the mansion. "Did you know what I was from the beginning? Is what I am the reason we are together?"

"No!" Antoine strides forward and clasps my face in his

hands, his eyes searching mine. "No, Harper. I swear to you. If you believe nothing else, please believe that." I can feel the heat of his hands, the strength in them despite the gentleness with which he holds my face. It's hard being so close to him. Despite myself, my body is reaching toward his, the depths of his eyes pulling me in. I want to believe him. But Connor's words touched a deep ravine of insecurity somewhere inside me, gave voice to the fear I have been trying to suppress ever since Antoine came back.

I step back, so his hands fall away. "I need some time," I say quietly. "And I need to work out how to get my brother back, Antoine."

I turn and walk away, aware he is watching me go. But he doesn't follow me, and despite what I just said, a part of me wishes he would.

When day breaks, neither Tate nor Antoine are in the mansion. It's Saturday. Sometime midmorning I'm hit with a huge wave of exhaustion, the events of the past few days catching up with me. I sleep all day, wake for long enough to make some instant soup, and fall back to sleep. The gray light of dawn is creeping through the window when I finally wake on Sunday, feeling clearer and more positive than I have in days.

I shower and wash my hair, combing the tangles out. I stare at the long mass in the mirror when I get out. I've never thought of it before, but my hair truly is wild. Mom always said my and Tessa's hair was like an untamed garden. She threatened to cut our hair a thousand times when we were young, but she never followed through. My hair was past my waist before the end of elementary school and has only gotten thicker and curlier with time.

Now I stare at it and wonder if even my hair is a sign of what is inside me.

Annoyed at my own fancy, I twist the unruly mass into a ruthless knot on top of my head and turn my back on my own reflection.

When I come downstairs the front door is, as always, standing open, and I see three vehicles turning in through the gates at the bottom of the drive. The first is Avery's. I can see her and Jeremiah in the front. Behind that is a truck I don't recognize, with Louisiana plates. And behind that, making my heart leap with joy, is Connor's truck.

I stand on the porch nursing my coffee as they all pull up. Avery returns my greeting with notable reserve and without her usual hug. Jeremiah gives me a crooked smile, but I sense in him a similar reserve. Seeing Avery looking me up and down when she thinks I don't notice, I sigh inwardly. Connor has clearly told them about me. So much for keeping it quiet.

Connor hardly looks at me at all.

The Louisiana truck belongs to Remy. To my surprise, he seems the least affected by my new supernatural status, bounding up the porch steps and thrusting his hand out for a hearty shake. "So," he grins broadly, "Deepwater's latest monster, huh? Gotta say you don't seem too scary to me, Harper."

"Given that the most dangerous thing I can do is grow plants, I should think not."

Remy winks at me. "There's a few weed dealers on my side of the river would think that was plenty helpful. You're ever stuck for cash, you let me know."

I can't help but return his smile. There's something likeable about Remy, even if he is, clearly, a reprobate of the first order.

"We didn't come here for a social chat." Connor's face is grim and cold as Antoine's when he is angry. I sigh inwardly and wonder how it is that the two men I love the most in the world both have the ability to throw up emotional walls that could rival the height and strength of the Romans'.

"Your brother here has a plan in mind." Despite the early hour, Remy pulls a beer from the refrigerator and flips the cap off, sitting down uninvited at our kitchen table. Putting his feet up on it, he takes a long pull on the beer and fixes me with a pointed stare. "You won't like it."

My eyes swivel to Connor, who is standing in the doorway with his arms folded. I wait.

"Remy's mom, Lori, has helped me connect with Noya's spirit," says Avery. She exchanges a look with Jeremiah, who nods as if to encourage her. "Noya has helped us to understand a little more about the wolves."

"We thought it was a clan thing, you see." Remy picks up where she left off. "And it is, for the most part. The only people to turn into wolves are all connected to the same lineage, the last descendants of one of the Sun families, a rival clan to your friend Tate's. We thought that meant we were born, not made, like your vamp friends are."

I get the beginning of a very bad feeling in my stomach.

"Turns out, though," Remy goes on, "that there is a way a wolf can be made."

"Well, according to legend." Avery shoots Remy a warning glance.

He shrugs and tips the rest of the beer down his throat, then helps himself to the bottle of rum on the shelf. "Before a few weeks ago, we were no more than legends either. I'd say your girl Noya, wherever she is now, has access to knowledge that ain't too easy to come by for the living."

"Is that right?" I ask Avery, looking at Jeremiah for confirmation when she nods. "Is Noya getting information from—spirits?" I feel stupid even saying it.

"It's hard to explain." Avery's eyes go slightly unfocused. "I can't always make a clear connection with her, and it isn't as if she speaks, as such. It's more a knowing: impressions, images, some snatches of words. From what I can make out, though, there was once a time when most of the clan were wolves. And occasionally, in very special circumstances, they inducted an outsider into their magic."

"An outsider." My eyes move to Connor, who stares back at me with the same cold expression, his arms still folded. "You," I say flatly. "You want to do this."

"It's the only way your brother here is going to get a chance at this Keziah creature." Remy seems not at all troubled by the tension. "Pathetic little human that he is, he can't touch her, and he sure can't rescue his girl Cass. But with a bit of wolf power—well." He bares his teeth in what I just know he would like me to think of as a wolfish smile. Unfortunately, the word fits. Even in his human form, Remy has a distinctly feral look about him. And I swear the bulging arm muscles have grown even more pronounced since the last time I saw him.

"There's just one catch." Jeremiah eyes me warily.

"Oh, there's a catch." I glare at him. "What a surprise."

"Noya can help me work some of the magic," Avery says. "But we'll need Antoine to help with the actual transition." She looks at me. "And according to Noya," she says slowly, "we need to make a particular herbal mixture, using moonflowers."

"Well, there's no shortage of those," I mutter, glancing at where moonvine curls over the Ionic columns.

"We also need you to mix it up." Connor speaks for the first time.

"Me?" I look at them, taken aback. "Why me?"

"Because according to the legends of our clan," says Remy, taking a swig of rum straight from the bottle, "this witchy little potion will only work if it's made by someone connected to earth magic."

"I'm not a witch," I say, in what is beginning to feel like an automatic response.

"Maybe not." Remy raises his eyebrows at me. "But Avery can help with the how. It's the what that we need. You better hope they're right about that magic in your veins, magnolia girl."

"Why?" I look at Connor.

"Because," says Remy, "turns out, wolves have one thing in common with vamps." He tips the bottle up again and swallows, holding my eyes. "They have to be more or less dead to turn."

CHAPTER 11

FRIENDS

"More or less dead."

I repeat the words slowly, staring at Connor. He stares right back.

"Like Cass was more or less dead? Because that wasn't more or less, Connor. That was *dead*. What are you trying to say here?"

"Well the fact is, none of us really know, being kind of new to this and all." Remy swings his legs off the table and looks out the window. "But I know who might." He grins at me as the sound of Antoine's truck comes roaring up the driveway. I stifle a sigh. From the pace of the truck, it sounds like Antoine is already aware of why I have visitors.

Two doors slam closed. Tate is with him, then. For two people who have kept communication to a minimum for three centuries, I think, they seem remarkably unconcerned by the amount of time they are suddenly spending together. Despite all the tension between Antoine and me, I can't help but feel glad about that. I wonder if they aren't both secretly grateful for the crisis that has caused them both to return home, and to one another.

They appear in the kitchen barely a moment after the slamming doors. *We've all become accustomed to weird,* I think. Nobody even pretends to be human, anymore.

"Would someone care to explain why Remy's mother seems to think there will soon be another wolf running around the bayou?" Antoine's tone is deceptively calm, but the hard golden gleam in his slate eyes is one I know all too well. Tate stands at his side, and for once, there is no trace of warmth on his face, either.

"I suggest you start talking," Tate says in an equally grim tone, looking first at Remy then at Connor.

"Told you they wouldn't like it." Remy, looking entirely unconcerned, throws the bottle of rum to Connor, who catches it neatly in one hand. "Here. You look like you're going to need this."

But Connor doesn't open it, I notice, with a sneaking sense of relief. At least he's making decisions sober. Then I remember the decision we're talking about and close my eyes. I'd almost prefer it if he were drunk. I open my eyes to find Remy looking at me quizzically. "Maybe it's you who needs to drink, magnolia girl."

"Don't call her that." Antoine's voice is like a whiplash.

"Why not?" Searching around for another bottle and not finding one, Remy takes another beer and sits back down at the table. There's a certain insolence in his gaze when he meets Antoine's eyes. "Thought you were planning to leave town, anyhow." He tips his beer up without losing eye contact, lips slightly curled around the bottle head.

Jeremiah makes a derisive noise. Antoine's gaze shifts to him, his eyes narrowing. "I had thought you of all people would have more sense than to be involved with this idiotic plan," Antoine says coldly.

Entirely undaunted, Jeremiah shrugs. "Cass was my friend long before you ever came to town. I don't want to see her become Keziah's killing machine. If there's a way to save her, then I'm all in."

"What makes you think you can save her?" Tate asks Connor. "Even if, by some miracle, you actually manage to become a wolf rather than dying—which, by the way, is highly improbable. As far as I can tell, the wolves have been doing the best they can to corral Keziah and her companions for weeks now. And yet they're still turning up to class and roaming the bayous, feeding on whomever they choose with impunity."

"Ah, but you see, that's because we've been trying to catch Keziah," says Remy. "That girl is wicked fast. Cass, on the other hand, is still new. Hasn't got quite the same skills. And none of your kind have the same strength or smarts as Keziah. Cass we can catch."

"If you can catch her," says Antoine with exaggerated patience, "then why haven't you?"

Remy tilts his head at Connor.

"Because to catch her," my brother says flatly, "they have to bite her. And I made it very clear that if any of them even thought of doing that, I'd kill them."

"You threatened werewolves. How intelligent of you." Antoine gives my brother a hard look, then throws Remy a scathing glance. "And you listened to him?"

Remy half smiles. "What can I say? I'm a romantic."

Antoine looks back at Jeremiah. "You need to stay out of all this," he says.

"Why?" Jeremiah meets his eyes steadily. "Because I'm the last living Marigny? It doesn't matter anymore. There's no binding that needs our name, or my blood. And even if there was—you have Harper now. And as it turns out, Harper is not just a helpless human. If what Remy's mom says is right, she might turn out to be just as powerful as you, in her own way." When Antoine doesn't immediately answer, Jeremiah's mouth twists. "I think it's about time you started realizing that you don't control what is going on here anymore, Antoine. Your control ended the day Keziah got out of that cellar. Now Avery can talk to dead people. Cass is a vampire. And Harper is some kind of spirit that none of us even understand." His face has a determined set to it that is strangely reminiscent of Antoine's own. "You can't manage us all anymore, Antoine. Everyone here is involved, whether you like it or not. We all have a right to play the roles we can, or at least to have an opinion. All you can do is offer what help you can—or walk away." His eyes slide to me, then back to Antoine. "And we both know you aren't going to walk away. If you were, you'd already be gone. You couldn't leave Harper even if you wanted to. Maybe it's time you accepted the fact that you're actually married, and start being a husband, instead of fooling yourself that you're going to leave."

An awkward silence follows these words. I can't look at Antoine. Tate is staring diplomatically out the door. Remy, who seems highly amused, is watching us all with the same insolent grin.

It's Connor who finally breaks the silence.

"Frankly, I could care less about your marriage." He casts Antoine a dark look. "As far as I'm aware, it's still possible for me to rescind your invitation. You can either help—or get out of my house." The hard edge to his words hurts more than I could have imagined.

"There's no need. I was just leaving." Antoine's eyes pass over me without seeming to pause. "None of you have any idea what you are playing with," he says bleakly. "None."

Turning, he walks slowly out the door and takes the steps in one fluid leap. A moment later he is gone, and we are left standing in the kitchen, staring at one another.

CHAPTER 12

KIN

"I take it that staying means you don't agree with your brother." Remy grins provocatively at Tate. "Oh, wait —is Antoine actually your brother? I never really quite got that story."

"Those wolves you run with," says Tate quietly. "One of them, Henri, you call brother. Yet as far as I can discover, you don't have so much as a shared parent."

For the first time Remy's smile fades, replaced by a hard stare. "Henri and I are family," he says coldly. "Have been since the day my mother brought him home. And he's kin, somewhere back in history. Otherwise he wouldn't have become wolf."

"Well then," says Tate calmly. "I'm sure you understand that kin is not always so simple as people like to make it."

It's the first time I've seen Remy disconcerted. Tate turns to Connor. "I take it that both Remy's mother, and, through Avery, Noya too, have made it clear that this is a very dangerous and risky path to take. I've never seen magical shape-shifting done. I don't know anyone who has seen it. In fact, until Remy and his clan turned the night of the party, I would have believed the Natchez wolves entirely extinct."

"But Noya is with our ancestors now. And I believe her, Tate." Avery goes to stand at Remy's side. His arm snakes around her waist, pulling her in to stand between his thighs, her hand resting on his shoulder. Jeremiah shifts uncomfortably. Avery shoots me a slightly defiant look, as if daring me to say something. "I can feel them," she says, turning back to Tate. "Our entire line of ancestors—I can feel them. Ever since Remy brought me to his side of the river. It's like two pieces of myself fit together. All the strange things I've seen or heard over the years, things I just dismissed as tricks of the light or an odd whistle of wind—they've become clear for the first time. If this was wrong, if we couldn't do it, I would know. But we can do this, Tate. And for some reason, I truly think it's what they want."

I can feel Connor watching me.

"But you need me." I look at my brother, my voice flat. "Moonflowers are poisonous. You're asking me to mix a potion that is designed to kill you."

Remy's index finger points up from Avery's waist. "A potion that *could* kill him," he corrects. "We'll bite him before that happens. Then your man Antoine will give him some of his blood. Connor will drink from the wolf that bit him. Add a bit of full moon power and—*voila!* Your brother is a wolf boy, just like us."

"I can't believe it is that simple." I glance at Tate. "And Antoine will never agree. You heard him." Despite the words tasting like ash in my mouth, I say, "Wouldn't your blood work, Tate? Atsila was your mother, after all."

"I don't think so." Tate shakes his head. "I think if that kind of power ran in my veins, I would know it. My mother was famous, even in our tribe. It was said she not only knew the secrets of channelling power, but that she actually carried earth magic inside her. It was considered a rare and precious gift, one given by the gods, and not even in every generation. I never possessed anything like that." His face is grave, lost in the past, in memories. "We change when we're made, become something else. My mother sacrificed herself to Antoine. It's different to giving birth. She gave her life and with it, willingly gave Antoine her spirit, her knowledge—and her power. It was Antoine who caused the bayou wolves to turn, not I. If I had his power, I would have known it by now."

I don't want to delve too deeply into how he might know such a thing. Instead, I say,

"Does that mean Antoine's blood is different from that of other vampires? Contains special powers?"

Tate gives me a small smile, as if he knows what I'm not saying. "Noya had unerring instincts about our people and a great deal of knowledge. Antoine was made for a purpose, a conscious effort to make something strong enough to defeat Keziah. I can't communicate with our ancestors like Avery can, but if she says now that it is Antoine alone who can do this, then I would trust her."

"Antoine won't agree." I say it again, and Connor makes an impatient noise.

"He will if you ask him to, Harper."

Suddenly they're all staring at me. "That's not true," I say. "I don't have power over Antoine."

"Of course you do." Connor's tone is clipped and curt. "Antoine is in love with you."

"I thought you said it was my so-called powers he was in love with?" I can't disguise the hurt in my voice.

"Either way." I flinch at the coldness in his response. "You're the only thing Antoine cares about. The only thing he'd die to protect. If you ask him, he'll do it."

"What makes you think I will do it?" I stare at him. "You're asking me to make the means of your death, Connor. You of all people know what you're asking. You're the only family I have left."

"And you owe me this." Connor strides across the kitchen to stand directly in front of me, eyes blazing. "Whether you meant to or not, the secrets you kept, the lies you told, are what led to this. Cass is dead because you and Antoine thought you could manage this between yourselves." His voice is remorseless as a dentist's drill on a nerve. "Well—you were wrong. And Jeremiah is right: we're all involved now, whether you like it or not. It isn't a question of whether we're messing with things we don't understand, as Antoine said. The truth is that whether we like it or not, those things we don't understand have us all caught up, and unless we try to take control of them, we'll all die because of what we don't understand."

Connor shakes his head, his face hard and hurt. "We can't just pretend none of this is happening. We can't keep Cass's mother, or the teachers at your school, compelled forever. People are already talking, wondering what's going on with Cass. She's dangerous, and at the moment, she's completely under Keziah's control. I don't know what Keziah's ultimate plan is—but I don't see it ending well for Cass." He puts his hands on my shoulders. "I love you, Harper," he says, and his voice breaks on the words. "You're my family. But I love Cass, too. Since Mom and Tessa died, loving Cass is the first time I felt like I had a whole heart again, a real reason to actually live. If she dies because there was something I could have done and didn't—" his voice breaks off.

All I can hear is my own words when Tessa was dying. All I remember is how I felt when Connor begged me not to give our sister a kidney. It isn't fair. It isn't right.

But I understand it.

"Please, Harper." Connor's fingers dig into my shoulders, his eyes boring into mine. "Help me do this."

I look over his shoulder at Tate. "And you believe this will actually work?"

Tate lifts one shoulder with a pained expression. "There are never guarantees."

"If it doesn't work," I say flatly, "can you bring Connor back before the poison in the moonflowers kills him?"

Tate doesn't answer that. The pained expression on his face is answer enough.

"Antoine will never forgive me if I force his hand in this," I mutter.

"Yes, he will." Tate gives me a crooked smile. "I know a little about Antoine and his ability to forgive."

I shoot him a dirty look. "Unlike you, I don't have three centuries to waste while he thinks on it."

"Trust me." Connor shakes me gently. "Antoine will forgive you." His voice softens, and for the first time I see a hint of the brother I know in his eyes. "He does love you, Harper. I hate it, and God knows I don't understand it, not really. But he does."

From the corner of my eye I see Remy's arm tighten around Avery's waist, pulling her against him. Despite the unforgiving light in her eyes, the knowledge that there are things between us unsaid, I still trust Avery. "Can you really do this?" I ask her.

She nods slightly.

I take a deep breath.

"Okay." I look around the room. "I guess I'm in."

CHAPTER 13

SEEDS

I can't harvest the seeds of the moonvine until after dark.

"They lie dormant during the day," Avery tells me. "And we need to wait for the moon to shift into the sign of Leo."

"Why?" We're sitting on the slope by the river, pale winter sunlight glistening from the deep green leaves of a nearby laurel tree. I try not to look at the magnolia trees, still blazing with flowers. Remy's teasing has made me uncomfortably aware of their rich, unseasonal growth. I pluck a leaf from the moonvine and tear it into small pieces. When I throw them at the river, they just flutter into the air or stick to my hand, not going anywhere.

"Do you know what the traditional name is for the January full moon?" Avery asks.

I shake my head.

"The Wolf Moon. It was called that because years ago, people would hear wolves howl beneath it. You need to wait until the moon moves into the constellation of Leo, the sign of the lion, before harvesting the seeds from the moonvine for the potion. Leo is the wildest and most powerful of animal signs, the best one to use for work such as this. We'll pick the seeds as soon as the moon shifts sign, then wait until it reaches its zenith to work the magic of Connor's transformation." Avery is animated when she talks about the process.

"You seem to know a lot about it."

"Remy's mom has been teaching me. And then there's Noya."

"She talks to you often?"

"More than I would like, sometimes." Avery tears apart a leaf of her own. "There is something she said that is useful, though. A recipe for a tincture she wants me to drink. It can help me protect Connor during the ceremony. Noya said it would work best if you made it for me."

"Of course." I grasp at the chance to do something that might help. "Anything."

"You said once that you have night jasmine in your garden, seeds your sister gave you."

"I do."

"And it's flowering now?" I can't help but notice the careful manner in which she asks.

"Yes." I look at her slightly defiantly. "Night jasmine blooms in winter, you know."

"Of course." Avery nods a little too readily, her cheeks suspiciously ruddy under her tawny skin. "Anyway, you'll need some of the flowers, and a couple of seeds. I can write the instructions down for you. I've brought the rest of the ingredients with me." She looks sideways at me. "Tonight is about Connor," she says quietly. "Night jasmine is poison, but it's also a potent shield, used the right way. And seeds that belonged to your sister, planted by you— nothing could be better designed to protect him." She smiles crookedly at me. "And we need every ounce of protection we can find. If there's magic in those hands of yours, Mrs. Marigny, I'm having me a piece of it." I'm taken aback at the use of my married name, but seeing her sly smile, I can't help but laugh—and somehow laughing makes the ring on my finger gleam in a happy way, and some of the darkness that seems to surround my marriage dissipates into the night.

"What are they like, the wolves?" I'm genuinely curious. "I've never seen a wolf in the wild in Mississippi. I always thought they were a cold climate kind of thing."

"They're called red wolves. And they're nearly extinct. Just like the Natchez, they've been hunted almost out of existence." I hear the note of bitterness in Avery's voice. How must it be, I wonder, to discover such a rich heritage, and yet have almost nobody left to ask about it?

"Is Remy—are the Natchez wolves the same as those found in the wild?"

"Kind of. They're bigger, darker. And faster. Which means they have to stay hidden. If anyone finds them, they'll become a lab experiment nobody will be able to explain." She glances sideways at me. "They've already risked a lot trying to rescue Cass. Keziah has come close to killing some of them more than once."

I get the feeling that by some of them, she means Remy.

"You and Remy," I say. "Are you . . . ?"

"I'm not sure what we are, yet." Avery gives me a half smile, the closest she's come since her arrival to the lighthearted girl I used to know. "I guess that's a common problem around here, huh."

"That's an understatement." I smile ruefully. "Avery," I say hesitantly, "I'm sorry I didn't tell you about all of this." I gesture at the night garden. "I only found out myself recently. And I still don't understand, really, what it is or what it means. What I am. I wasn't trying to keep anything from you."

"I know that." Avery looks away. "I guess it's just that ever since Antoine came back, it's as if you live in this closed-off little world. One that only you, Antoine, and Tate seem to understand. The rest of us are just—cut off. I know you don't mean to do it. You're one of the least selfish people I know. It's just that, I guess, you lived in a secret world for so long before anybody else became part of it, sometimes it feels as if that world is yours, and nobody can enter. Not me, with this ability I sometimes honestly wish I didn't have, to hear and see things I don't really understand. Not poor Cass, who I think actually suspected something was going on long before anyone else. Not even your brother, who I know you love. And now Remy and the wolves . . . can you even imagine how life-changing this has been for them? I know Remy seems tough, like nothing bothers him, but now he's responsible for an entire clan of wolves—men who were unstable even before they found themselves becoming something supernatural. And still it seems like you, Antoine, and Tate hold all the power, make all the decisions. The rest of us are just dependent on your agreement to do anything. I guess I resent that, if I'm honest."

I stay silent for a while, digesting her words. I'm not sure what to say, or even how I feel.

"Anyway." She pats my arm. "It's okay."

"No, Avery. It isn't. And I'm so sorry that's how it seems." I meet her eyes. "I wish I could tell you something that could make it better. But the truth is, I don't understand any of this any more than you can. I found myself neck-deep in it all before I really knew how it happened." I stare out over the river, the landscape blurring before my eyes. "My life isn't even recognizable anymore. Once, I thought I'd become an artist, maybe have a nursery that sold flowers and plants. Something peaceful and quiet that meant I could stay close to Connor. I even dreamed of meeting a man I loved, of getting married and having children." The pale winter sun glints on the water, the air hard and lonely around me. "Now," I say slowly, "I'm married to the one man who can never give me children. I love Antoine so much I can't bear to even think of life without him. But I spend every waking moment terrified he is going to leave, that I'll never see him again." I shake my head, aware of how maudlin I sound. Striving for a lighter tone, I go on: "On top of that, I'm apparently some kind of magical creature who could possibly pose a risk to everyone I love. I guess you're right about me being at the center of a strange world. But I never planned to be here. And I'd do anything to take back what has happened to Cass, and to Remy."

"I know." Avery smiles at me. "But don't worry too much about Remy. To be honest, I think he's pretty happy to be a wolf. In some weird way it's given his life meaning." She leans a little closer. "His mother admitted to me that until this happened, she was fairly sure he'd end up dead or in jail. Now he can't risk getting jailed, because he can't risk exposing himself as a wolf, or any of the others. I think it's the most law-abiding he's been in his life."

"And he's definitely hot," I say, now that we're laughing.

"So hot." Avery rolls her eyes. "You should see him without clothes—"

"Avery!"

"Oh, come on. Are you trying to tell me you and vamp boy still haven't . . . ?"

"Actually—no. We haven't." My face heats up and I look down at the ground.

"Seriously?" I can hear the incredulity in her tone. "But the way he looks at you—the way he kisses you, for goodness' sake! And besides, you're actually married to him, Harper. Even the church can't argue with that."

"Well, technically, our marriage can still be annulled." I'm so mortified I can barely look at her. "And I think Antoine wants to keep that option open . . . which is why he won't . . . why we haven't," I finish lamely.

"You think he wants an escape clause?"

I nod. I'm about to say more when a movement behind us causes us both to swing around, and my already-red face goes up in flames. Antoine is standing barely feet behind us. There's no way he didn't hear that conversation.

"Avery," he says quietly, "do you mind giving me a moment with Harper?"

Avery is already scrambling to her feet, as embarrassed as I am. She says something about going to find Remy and gets out of there so fast I almost smile.

Antoine sits on the grass next to me. Picking up one of the moonflowers from the ground, he hands it to me with a small smile. "So this weed you're so fond of has some kind of purpose, after all."

"I'm not so sure about that." I turn the flower over between my fingers. "If taking my brother to the point of death is a purpose then yes, I suppose it does."

"But you're going to do it anyway."

I meet his eyes. "Yes," I say quietly. "I have to, Antoine. He's right. I owe him this much." I touch his arm. "But I am sorry for putting you in this position, for forcing your hand."

"How do you know I will help?"

The sunlight catches the gold flecks in his eyes, but they aren't hard and cold anymore. They're sun on sea again, the man I married on a magnolia-filled day. "Because I know you won't let Connor die," I say. "It's not who you are."

"You seem very sure of that. There are plenty who would tell you otherwise. Your brother included."

"Connor didn't mean what he said earlier. He's just hurt and angry."

"What about you?" Antoine brushes a stray curl behind my ear. "Do you think I married you because of this power you have?"

"No." It's only when I say it aloud that I realize I've known all along I don't believe it. "But I wish you'd told me what you suspected. I wish you'd just been honest with me."

He nods. "I do want to tell you the truth," he says. "About a lot of things. But I really don't want to speculate on what I don't know. And right now, Harper, please believe me—I don't know the whole truth of what you are, though I am doing everything I can to find out." He takes my hand, turning it over in his own. "I have to ask a favor," he says, glancing at me warily. "One I know you're not going to like. I wish I could explain it to you, but for now, it's a hunch, nothing more, and I don't want to tell you until I know for certain." He examines my eyes. "Will you trust me?" he says, "One last time? Then after this night is done, and I am certain, I promise I will tell you everything I know."

"You promise."

He holds up our hands, threading our fingers so the Marigny emerald gleams next to his plain wedding band. "I promise," he says again.

I nod slowly. "In that case, what is it that you want?"

He holds up a syringe. "Some of your blood."

I'm so taken aback I don't know what to say.

"Not much." His eyes hold mine. "And I need you to promise that you won't tell anyone. Not even Avery or Connor."

"What about Tate?"

He looks away for a moment. "Tate already knows."

"You trust Tate with this," I say. "But not me? Not my brother, who is risking his life tonight?"

"Harper." He holds my face, forcing me to look at him. "Believe me when I say there is nobody I trust more than you. And I don't mean any disrespect to Connor. But if something should go wrong tonight, if either of you should somehow fall into Keziah's hands—then the less you know, the better."

Eventually I sigh and put out my arm. "Go on, then."

I wait until the needle pierces my skin before I speak. "You know I'm going to be there tonight. With Connor."

"No, you're not." He wipes my arm with a cotton ball and carefully places a bandage over it. "You aren't going to be anywhere near it."

"That's the price of my blood," I say. "I'm making the potion, remember. And Connor is my brother. I'm going to be there. Otherwise you can hand that syringe back right now, and tell me what is going on."

"You think you can take the syringe from me." He's grinning, and my mouth twitches despite myself.

"I can make you give it to me."

"Oh, is that right?" His smile fades, and he holds my hand again. "Please stay away from danger tonight, Harper." I'm aware that his customary note of command is absent. He's trying. Albeit in a very Antoine manner, but he *is* trying. "I know you want to help your brother. But it truly will be dangerous, and it's better if you're nowhere near Keziah."

"I'll think on it." Although a dark cloud crosses his face, he doesn't push it, and I'm grateful. "Now leave me alone," I say, smiling at him nonetheless. "I need to work out this potion everyone seems so certain I'm able to make."

CHAPTER 14

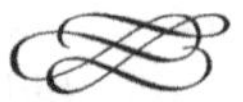

POTION

The moon shifts into the sign of Leo at twilight, rising soon after dusk. It seems apt that it is the moon of the lion under which Connor plans to become a wolf.

I begin Avery's night jasmine tincture as the moon begins to show through the trees. I prepare it as she instructed, crushing the seeds carefully beneath the boughs of the live oak, until they are no more than powder. I mix the powder carefully into a glass bottle containing pure alcohol combined with filtered river water. I fix the lid as the gleaming disk beams through the tunnel of live oak in front of the mansion. I take the bottle down to the night garden as I begin harvesting the moonvine seeds from the teardrop-shaped pods.

"Keep the night jasmine tincture close as you make the potion," Avery had instructed. "It will protect you as you work." Indeed, the glass bottle seems to glow with an odd, incandescent light as I move among the moonflowers.

It isn't straightforward. The moonvine pods can only be harvested when they're brown, so any green ones must be left. I need approximately a cup full to make the potion, according to Avery. I don't have long to work. I have only a couple of hours to harvest the pods and make the potion before the moon reaches its zenith just after eleven p.m., and it will be time for Connor's transformation. There is little room for error.

I take pods from the vine around my window, as well as from the night garden. Many of the pods split as I pick them, spilling yellow seeds into the glass bowl I'm using to collect them. As I work I fall into a meditative rhythm, finding the touch of the flowers on my hand and their soft scent soothing. Not long after night falls, I've collected enough for our purpose.

Avery has given me instructions as to the making of the potion. I know she wanted to stay to keep an eye on me, but I don't want any witnesses to what I am doing. Somehow I know I need to do this by myself. If I truly do possess some kind of odd power, I will find it alone, in privacy, with no bystanders to make me self-conscious. I don't need Antoine to tell me tonight will be dangerous. Nobody really knows if this will work at all. I need to give Connor the best possible chance of success. I won't have it fail because I couldn't give this potion my full attention.

I use Mom's granite mortar and pestle to crush the seeds and a little river water to loosen the mixture. I'm working on an old tree stump that I used as one of the borders to my night garden. Moonvine grows around the base, and a red magnolia branch hangs over it from the trees at the edge of the lawn. As I work, magnolia petals fall silently to the grass nearby, their scent mingling with the acrid stench of the moonflower seeds.

When the seeds are completely crushed, I pour the contents of the mortar into an old cooking pot that was also Mom's, placing it on the gas burner I brought down from the house. I bring it to a simmer, careful not to boil it, then begin to add the other ingredients Avery directed: raw frankincense for protection, cumin seed oil for safe transition, and some other herbs to make the concoction drinkable. When it is thickening, I go to the night garden to cut the final ingredient required. I waited until night dew had settled on the purple wolfsbane, as Avery had instructed. It isn't the purple flowers I harvest, but the dark, coarse leaves. I carefully cut a full spiral head of them, shivering slightly as I do. I can feel the potency held within them. If the moonvine seeds are toxic, these leaves are pure death. They feel dark in my hand, malevolent almost. It seems strange that the same plant that's deadly to wolves is also used to create one. It is something to do with the flow of life and death, Avery said. For something to be born, something must first die. But because the wolves are living creatures rather than dead, Connor must transmute a part of himself rather than kill it. If moonflower is the poison that kills him, wolfsbane is the means by which his body knows what it will become. It's a delicate balance, just as the spiral shape of the leaf head is itself intricate, and perfect.

I turn down the flame and remove the pot from the heat as the moon rises over the mansion, gleaming down on my hands as I stir the dark liquid. The potion spins faster in the pot, making a funnel in the center. The tincture of night jasmine I made earlier casts a protective light from a nearby branch. Feeling a sudden sense of urgency, I reach for the wolfsbane and wince as the knife I used to cut it pricks my finger. Ignoring the pain, I tear the wolfsbane leaves one by one from the spiral and drop them into the funnel, watching as they are sucked into the depths below. I realize I'm humming quietly, a soft vibration that I can feel in the earth under my bare feet, earth that feels warm despite the winter chill on the air. When the last leaf drops, the liquid slows and gradually comes to stillness. My humming stops. When I peer into the pot, the leaves have disappeared. The potion is dark and still, with a strange sheen over the top.

I am at once tired and exultant. Whatever it is that I was supposed to do, it is done. Somewhere inside myself, I know it is done right.

I walk back up the lawn and into the mansion. Connor, Avery, Remy, and Jeremiah are waiting in the kitchen. They look up expectantly. I hand Avery the bottle with her protective tincture and in my other hand hold up the pot of potion.

"It's done," I say.

THE PLACE OF CEREMONY IS ACROSS THE BRIDGE IN LOUISIANA, ON a clearing by the river, an old site sacred to Remy's clan. Antoine and Tate, I understand, are already there, meeting with Remy's mother. Connor hugs me goodbye on the porch.

"You don't have to do this." I cling to him, feeling the frantic trip of his heart through the thin shirt.

"Yes, I do." I feel his words against my hair. "You know I do." After a moment I nod, and finally I let him go, forcing a watery smile.

"I wish I could be there."

"I don't want you there." He shakes his head decisively. "As soon as it's done, Remy's pack and I are going after Keziah, using the element of surprise. Antoine and Tate are tracking her so we know where to go. They can't focus on the chase and look after you, too."

"I know." I touch his cheek. "Just be safe."

"Thank you for doing this." He holds up the old jam jar into which I've poured the potion. It seems a rather mundane receptacle for such a deadly thing, but it was all I had. The liquid inside is deep indigo. Rich—and lethal. I imagine it entering Connor's veins and shiver involuntarily.

A muscle twitches in his cheek. "I know you didn't want to make it. I won't forget it."

"If it means you will come back to me, then it's worth it." I hug him one last time. "Be safe," I say again, stepping away as he leaves me on the porch.

I wrap my shawl around me as they pile into vehicles and drive away. Jeremiah comes to stand next to me. "Thank you for staying." I shoot him a grateful look. "I didn't want to be alone tonight."

"It isn't like I'd be anything but a liability." There's a touch of bitterness in his voice. "But you're welcome." Jeremiah forces a smile that doesn't reach his eyes. I know it's hard for him. After tonight, he will be the only one of us all who is simply human. That can't be easy—nor can seeing Avery with Remy. I know Jeremiah has had a thing for Avery as long as I've known him. I'm not sure Avery has ever even been aware of it.

I sit down on the porch steps, and Jeremiah sits beside me. "I thought you would insist on going with them tonight."

"I wanted to." I stare down the tunnel of live oak, through which I can see the headlights racing down the road beyond. "But Antoine can't help Connor rescue Cass and protect me at the same time. There's no way I'm doing anything that might jeopardize Connor's chances of getting Cass back."

"But you wish you were there."

"So much."

"Me, too." We sit there in silence for a while, then Jeremiah fetches the rum bottle. We pass it back and forth in silence. It's just past nine o'clock.

CHAPTER 15

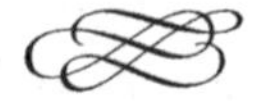

TURNED

Jeremiah's drunk a quarter of the bottle and I barely a glass, when my bare feet suddenly tingle. "Did you feel that?" I look down at the ground, trying to work out if it's just the rum or something else.

"I gotta be honest, Harper. I'm not feeling much." Jeremiah is slurring his words slightly. I get another odd vibration and leap up, staring at the ground beside the stairs.

"I definitely felt something that time." I walk downstairs and my feet seem to find their own path, leading me away to the left of the house.

"Hey, Harper!" Jeremiah lurches to his feet and stumbles after me. "I don't think you should leave the house." I know he's right. It isn't a night for exploring. I stop where the light from the house ends, my bare feet curling into the earth, trying to work out what it is I can feel.

"It's as if something is moving under the ground." I kneel down, putting both palms on the soil. This time it's more definite, like a tremor, as if the earth itself is shivering.

"Harper." There's suddenly no trace of drunkenness in Jeremiah's voice. "Where you're standing—isn't that one of the tunnels that leads to your cellar?"

I leap back as if I've been stung, and we stare at each other. He's right. I even know exactly which tunnel it is. It's where Antoine drank my blood, the night Keziah and Caleb almost escaped.

"What if Keziah knows you're here alone?" Jeremiah glances around warily. "We need to get out of here, Harper. Right now."

I don't stop to argue. I grab my Ariats from the bottom of the stairs and run for my Mustang, grateful I'm so lax with security that I leave my keys in the ignition, mainly so I don't lose them. I'm already turning the key when Jeremiah leaps in. The wheels spin in the gravel and the Mustang fishtails onto the driveway, picking up speed quickly. I glance in the rearview mirror as we near the gate, just in time to see a solid, bulky figure fill the doorway.

"Caleb," I mutter, as the convertible almost goes on two wheels around the corner. "Keziah sent Caleb here to get me."

"Which means Keziah is with Cass," says Jeremiah.

"Maybe." My mind is racing. "Or maybe she's sent Cass to be bait somewhere else. The real question is, where is Keziah—and what does she want?"

It isn't a question either of us can answer. I have no idea what the right thing to do is, but Jeremiah must be in the same mind frame as me, because when I turn across the bridge heading for Louisiana, he doesn't object.

Jeremiah directs me to the place on the bayou where the ceremony is going to take place. About a mile away, I pull up on the roadside. "I don't want to just show up." I look at Jeremiah, seeing my own worry reflected in his face. "I don't want to do anything that will distract their attention and put Connor in danger."

"We can't just sit here. Caleb will be looking for us." Jeremiah glances fearfully over his shoulder. "He could have called Keziah, told her what happened."

"I don't think he can talk."

"Text?" Jeremiah says doubtfully. I shrug. Truth is, I have no idea how Caleb and Keziah communicate, or even if they do. All he's ever been to me is her silent shadow, menacing and at the same time, not quite real. It's odd, I think, how unless someone actually communicates, even silently, it's hard to imagine them as an actual person. Caleb seems unreal to me, insubstantial, more *thing* than man.

But that doesn't mean I'm not scared of him. I'm also surprised he let us go. I've seen how fast Antoine can move. If Caleb had wanted to stop us driving away, he could have. He let us escape, and I'm not sure why.

"Is there somewhere near the site where we can see Connor and the others, but not be seen? Where we could hide the car?"

"Sure there is." Jeremiah rolls his eyes. "It's the bayou, Harper. More things are hidden there than anyone likes to think about."

We carry on down the back roads until we near the site, then roll the car into a mass of palmetto and cypress growing thick along the soft edge of the bayou. I eye the Mustang doubtfully and hope we don't have to leave in a hurry. I suspect it may take a tow rope and Connor's truck to get it out again. Jeremiah and I creep through the thick undergrowth and soft ground toward the clearing. Soon the gathering comes into sight, and we duck down, about a hundred yards from where Connor, clad in only a pair of denim shorts, is kneeling on the ground. Avery and a tall woman I assume is Lori are in front of him, Antoine behind. I look at my phone; it's eleven o'clock.

A moment later, there is a rustle in the undergrowth, and I swing around, my heart pounding, Jeremiah equally tense beside me. Topaz eyes gleam at us through the bushes. I freeze, unsure whether to scream or not. Then the leaves part, and a large, dark wolf emerges to stand in front of us. It's jowls part, and for a moment I would swear it is grinning at me.

Remy.

He stares at us for a moment, then bounds over our heads and into the clearing. Antoine swings around as he does, only relaxing when he sees what—or who—it is. "You're late," I hear him say tersely, as Remy pads across the ground. The other wolves emerge from the trees around the clearing, and I guess that they've been running the perimeter of the area, ensuring it's secure. Now they form a circle around Connor, Avery, Lori, and Antoine. Remy, the only wolf inside the circle, stands at Antoine's side. His mother stands on the other side of him. Lori is strongly built, with handsome, angular features and direct eyes the deep brown of molasses.

Lori looks up at the sky and says, "It's time." I feel a queer jolt somewhere inside. The moon must have reached it's zenith, I realize. I wonder that I've never noticed before how that feels. Perhaps it's simply that I've never paid attention.

I can't hear what Lori and Avery are saying, but they're standing over Connor. Avery raises the tincture and drinks it down, shuddering as she does, then passes it to Lori, who does the same. Avery takes a deep breath, then places her hands on Connor's heart. Lori places hers on his head. The two women begin chanting in low, hypnotic voices, a rhythmic sound that starts quietly then grows, becoming more intense.

Without pausing her chanting, Lori holds out her hand, and Antoine passes her the wolfsbane potion. She unscrews the lid and holds it up to the moon. Even from a distance, I see the dark, shiny liquid begin to move in the jar, slowly at first, then picking up speed, so it is swirling in a dark, silent spiral as Lori slowly lowers the jar into Connor's hands. Her voice picks up, though I still can't make out what she says, and I become aware that I am humming just as I did in the garden earlier, the same odd, tuneless sound I made when I mixed the potion. Connor tips his head back, opens his mouth, and pours the dark, spinning liquid into it.

For a moment nothing happens. He gulps the liquid down, and I see him shudder, as if his body wants to retch and he is forcing it under control. Avery's hands are on either side of his body now, as if she cradles his heart in them, her and Lori's chanting growing louder. I can feel it in my body, my humming joining their voices as if we are one.

Then Avery and Lori simultaneously call out, a sudden, hoarse cry, and lift their hands, falling away from Connor's body. Remy leaps forward. I have to put a hand over my mouth to stifle my scream as his jaws open and crush closed on Connor's torso, tearing the flesh savagely from his heart, across his shoulder, to behind his shoulder blade. Connor makes no sound, and I can't see his face. Remy releases him and my brother falls forward with dull finality, collapsing facedown on the earth.

The night feels still and charged, taut with energy. I'm scared to so much as breathe. Antoine kneels down. He places one hand beneath Connor's heart, the other on his back, and takes up the chant where Avery and Lori left off, a low, soothing stream of words that I know comes from Atsila, the medicine woman inside him. Gently he raises Connor's torso. Without missing a word, he tears the skin of his wrist open with his teeth, lowering it to Connor's mouth. The blood drips in a steady stream, falling down the side of Connor's mouth.

But my brother doesn't move.

There is silence in the clearing. Beside me Jeremiah is still as stone, riveted by the scene before us. The wolves look on expectantly. Is it my imagination, or do they begin to turn to one another, as if doubting? Lori looks down at the ground. Avery's hands are clasped together. She stares at Connor's prone body, her face pale. Antoine gently lays Connor down and steps away. His face is grave. He looks at Remy, and even from here, I can see the worry in his face. It isn't working, I think, my heart sinking. Antoine thinks Connor is going to die.

Remy sniffs around the still body on the grass, snuffling the head, the loins, the feet, whimpering. I taste sick dread in my mouth. The wolf turns his back on Connor, his tail between his legs. He looks toward where Jeremiah and I crouch, his topaz eyes gleaming with what I know is sympathy.

Jeremiah reaches out and takes my hand. I let him. We stay crouched, staring at the still tableau in the center of the clearing.

For a long moment nothing moves.

Then, as one, the wolves seem to shiver. Remy's tail goes stiff behind him, and he growls, low in his throat. A moment later the circle of wolves are on their bellies, whining, as if they're in pain. Then Remy throws his head back, and from his throat rips an unearthly howl. The wolves crawl on their bellies toward Connor's fallen body, pushing Avery out of the way. Antoine steps back, frowning, as my brother's body disappears under the pack. Then they're all howling, a chilling, bloodcurdling sound that cuts the night.

A strange cry, strangled and small, breaks above their combined howls.

The cry deepens and thickens. Gradually swelling, it adds a deeper, somehow fiercer note to their collective chorus, and the circle of wolves come to their feet and back away, their howls gradually dying down.

Connor's body has gone. In its place stands a wolf, completely black where the others are burnished red, its eyes gleaming, crimson over gold, like the color deep in opal. It looks directly across the clearing to me, then calls once, commandingly. It leaps beyond the circle, running into the night, and the pack follows hard behind it.

Antoine looks around briefly, frowning at where we are hiding; then a savage cry echoes from the bayou, the wolf that is my brother calling for Antoine. My husband glances at my hiding place one last time then runs after my brother.

"It worked," I breathe, turning to Jeremiah. He nods.

My brother is a wolf.

CHAPTER 16

TENTACLES

"You shouldn't be here."

Jeremiah and I swing around to find Tate frowning at us. Back in the clearing, Lori is talking to Avery, their heads bowed together.

"We had to leave," Jeremiah says defensively. "Caleb came to the mansion. We only just got away."

"If Caleb had meant to capture you," says Tate, "you wouldn't have been able to get away. Which means he wanted you here." He puts hands on our shoulders and moves us into the clearing, not gently.

"They're close." Lori seems unsurprised to see us. "Keziah has us surrounded." She nods at Avery, who looks both scared and determined. "It's time for you to do what we spoke about. As for you," she goes on, gesturing to Jeremiah and I, "you need to drink the rest of that." She nods at the tincture I prepared earlier. Avery unscrews the lid and wordlessly hands us the jar. Jeremiah drinks first, shuddering just as Avery had. I drink. The tincture slides down my throat, seeming at once to both coat the inside of my veins and set them alight.

"Stand here on either side of me." Lori takes our hands as we do what she asks.

I glance at Tate. "What about you?"

"I will stay here." His eyes search the perimeter of the clearing, and he moves about ten yards away from us. Avery begins to move around us, shaking something with one hand.

"Salt?" Jeremiah says, watching her. "Really? I thought that was just a myth." Avery is pouring the white grains on the earth as she walks, making a circle around us, leaving Tate on the other side.

"All myths come from somewhere." Lori is watching Avery. "Salt reduces water activity. Water is a conduit for energy, and the earth here holds a lot of water. Laying salt in a circle inhibits the flow of energy, temporarily at least, and so forms a barrier against those with the ability to manipulate it."

"Like Keziah?" I ask.

Lori shrugs. "Nobody understands what Keziah does, exactly. But salt may at least help keep her out of our heads." It's only as Avery closes the circle that I realize she has excluded herself, standing outside it with Tate.

"What about Avery?" says Jeremiah. "Isn't she the most susceptible to Keziah's mind control?"

"Avery can't protect the wolves from inside the circle." Lori doesn't notice the color drain from Jeremiah's face. "Nor can she help Cass." Jeremiah and I exchange a glance, but neither of us say anything. This is Avery's choice, just as making the potion for Connor was mine. I don't like it any more than Jeremiah. But in Avery's shoes, I know I would have done the same, and I'm guessing Jeremiah would, too.

The circle is completed not a moment too soon.

A figure speeds out of the trees, and Cass is standing there, barely fifty yards from us. Her endless legs gleam beneath a red sheath dress that highlights the predatory color of her eyes. A black wolf emerges from the trees and she swings around, baring her teeth and snarling ferociously. The wolf that is Connor circles her cautiously, his own teeth bared as he growls low in the back of his throat. Antoine is right behind him, watching Cass warily.

I hear a shout of warning and turn to find Tate crouched in a similar fashion to Cass, facing Caleb's burly figure emerging on the opposite side of the clearing. Caleb's face is as bland and closed as ever. He walks slowly toward Tate, but his eyes are on me. I shiver as their cold, black depths seem to reach inside me, searching for something, like a noxious weed trying to find purchase among the flowers in my garden.

Lori's hand closes on mine. "Don't let him in." It isn't my imagination, I realize. Caleb is trying to break the salt barrier around us. I take a deep breath and focus all my energy on repelling the grasping sensation of his eyes.

"She's here," hisses Jeremiah from Lori's other side, and I wrench my eyes from Caleb's to follow his gaze. Keziah is standing on the edge of the clearing, forming the final point of a triangle made by her, Cass, and Caleb. Remy faces her and three other wolves circle behind her, whining uncomfortably. Remy himself is low to the ground, tail out flat behind him, growling as his bulk shifts with Keziah's every move. He is stalking her, blocking her advance, and when I see frustration flare in her eyes, I feel a rush of satisfaction. Maybe we have a chance, after all.

Keziah's eyes flicker to Avery, who clenches her fists, recoiling as if she's been hit. Avery's shoulders rise as she takes a deep breath. She releases it in a steady stream, and I can almost sense the protective tincture I made, settling around Remy and the wolves in a jasmine mist that seems to actually hang in the air, putting a barrier over the wolves just like the salt surrounding us. Keziah's eyes flash angrily. "Steady, Avery," murmurs Tate, moving in front of her, using his own body as a barrier between her and Keziah. He reels on his feet, and I can tell Keziah is throwing herself at him in some way, and that it is hurting him to repel her.

"Harper," mutters Jeremiah, and I turn to find Caleb has moved across the ground toward us. I can suddenly feel him, the insidious darkness of his eyes working like tentacles through the ground, trying to find a way under the salt and into us. I kick off my boots and feel the earth like a shock against my bare feet. I hold his eyes across the ground and breathe deep like Avery did, trying to feel the night jasmine in my blood, feel my way under the earth to the water there, to find where he is seeking us.

"Careful," hisses Lori. "He wants you to find him. Be careful, Harper."

I can hear Connor's growls increase, but staring at Caleb, I can't see him. "What's happening?" I ask Jeremiah through clenched teeth. I don't know what it is that Caleb's doing, but it feels as if it's taking every ounce of my concentration to keep his tentacles away from me.

"Connor is circling Cass, getting closer to her." I hear a sudden, short shriek of fury. "Cass doesn't like it," says Jeremiah, somewhat unnecessarily.

"What—about—Antoine," I pant. Caleb has just taken another step toward me. The sensation of tentacles reaching for me is more intense, almost unbearable now.

"He's coming around behind Cass." Jeremiah's voice is taut with excitement.

From the corner of my eye, I see Keziah lunge forward. She moves too fast for me to make out exactly what she's doing, but a moment later Remy tumbles through the air, yelping in pain, and I see Avery tremble as if she herself has taken a body blow.

"Antoine!" Keziah calls in a commanding tone. "You can't fight me, Antoine. Step aside." I shudder. I can almost feel the power in her summons, reaching for Antoine just as Caleb reaches for me.

"Antoine is fighting her," Jeremiah says. "He and Connor are closing in on Cass."

"They need to hurry." I grit my teeth as Caleb takes another step forward. With a brute gesture of her arm, Keziah dissipates Avery's jasmine mist, smiling coldly as she kicks the wolves aside.

"Don't you touch him," mutters Avery as Keziah advances on the prone wolf lying on the ground. Avery clenches her fists and inhales sharply. Remy gets unsteadily to his feet, shaking his head dazedly, and Avery hisses her breath out, sending another mist across the ground, just as I hear a sudden, savage snarl.

My concentration breaks and I swing around as Connor leaps for Cass's neck, sinking his teeth into her skin. Cass screams, a high, chilling sound, and stumbles, clearly hurt. She rips Connor from her neck and sends him hurtling across the ground and into a tree, where he falls dully to the ground. But Cass's strength is clearly waning fast, and she collapses with the effort of throwing Connor. Antoine lunges forward, clasping Cass in an iron-hard grip as he pierces her skin with the syringe. My blood disappears into her neck, and her body seems to go momentarily limp in Antoine's embrace.

Keziah cries out, a savage, unearthly cry that knocks Tate and Avery to the ground and buffets the air around us so it seems to ripple in dull waves, beating against the edges of Avery's salt circle and making the earth beneath my feet shudder. From the corner of my eye I see Connor quiver, then roll groggily to his feet. My attention snaps back into focus to find Caleb standing right before me, his feet almost touching the salt circle, his fathomless black eyes boring into me with the corrosive darkness of death itself, scratching at the edge of the salt from underneath, worrying at it like a dog gnawing a bone. Terrible fear grips me. I can't fight him. His eyes gleam and I know he can feel it too, how close he is.

Then Connor is there with two other wolves, leaping at

Caleb's throat. Caleb rounds on them, his mouth open in soundless cry, trying to beat them off, but Connor snarls savagely, leaping at him, trying to find purchase with his jaws. As Caleb twists this way and that, recoiling from Connor's relentless advance, another wolf leaps up from behind. The two bite down viciously, leaving raw, gaping holes in Caleb's arm and neck. As the vampire stares down at his arm in dull bemusement, I feel the grasping tentacles in the earth fade and recede. Connor looks up at me with dark eyes, then darts away, back to Cass.

Keziah shrieks again, but this time I hear the note of desperation in it. Suddenly she is no longer fighting off the wolves nearby or advancing on us. In a lightning movement she is at Caleb's side, and as she catches his huge, toppling form, she looks at me. I catch a glimpse of the expression in her eyes. With a shock, I recognize what it is: fear.

With one last backward glance at where Cass slumps against Antoine, Keziah makes another sound, this one of pain and loss; then she is gone, bearing Caleb's bulk as if he were no more than a child, streaking away to be swallowed by the bayou night.

Tate and Avery are already up, off the ground, moving swiftly to where a limping Connor prowls the ground beside Antoine, who holds Cass's prone form.

"Stay where you are," Lori orders as I begin to move. Her hand tightens on mine. "It's not over yet."

"I need to go to my brother."

"Cass is still dangerous. If she remains under Keziah's control, she may try to take you. Stay here."

Reluctantly I obey, though it hurts to watch Connor limp toward Antoine and Cass, to see the way he sniffs around Cass's prone figure, whining softly when she doesn't move. Then suddenly Cass is on her feet and Connor leaps back, balancing on his paws low to the ground, watching her with the same wary caution as everyone else.

"Cass." Antoine puts out his hand as one would to a wild animal. Cass spins to face him.

"What have you done to me?" I'm not sure if it's wishful thinking, but her voice, though still the high, clear voice of a stranger, seems gentler, less strident than before. More Cass, somehow.

"Can you still hear her? Keziah?" Antoine's question is low and calm, but I can hear the urgency beneath it.

"I can hear her. But not like before." Cass is staring at the black wolf before her. She takes a hesitant step toward it. "Connor?" she says, her voice breaking on the name. "Connor—is that you?" Her hand goes involuntarily to the wound on her neck, where Connor's teeth sank into her flesh. "What have you done to me?" I can hear the uncertainty in her voice. She looks around at us, her eyes wide with confusion and fear. "What happened to me? I don't understand."

"Okay," says Lori, letting go of our hands. "I think we're safe now."

"Wait," Antoine says, putting out a restraining hand. "First, Connor's blood."

My brother stands still, wild eyes watching Cass as Antoine's knife slashes a shallow wound in his shoulder. "Drink," Antoine commands her. Cass looks for a moment as if she might argue. Connor growls, a low sound of frustration. She glances at Antoine's face and back at Connor, then bends and puts her mouth to the cut.

Connor trembles at her touch, but he makes no sound at all as she draws his blood. She stands back, wiping her mouth, still watching Connor with a mixture of shame and defiance. Still he doesn't move, as if he's waiting for something.

"Now it's safe," says Lori.

Ignoring Antoine's grim face and unspoken warning, I race across the ground toward her, but Cass steps back, holding out a warning hand. "Don't," she says, shaking her head and looking at me with an expression somewhere between fear and fascination. "It isn't safe for me to be near you." I halt, unsure what to say. Cass turns to Avery. "Thank you," she says simply. "Whatever you did stopped Keziah. For long enough, at least." She touches the place on her neck where the syringe entered her and glances at me again. Then she looks at Antoine. "How long will it last? The blood? How long will it shield me from Keziah?"

Antoine lifts his shoulders. "I'm not sure." He looks at her closely. "If Keziah summons you again—"

"I can't fight her, Antoine. Not if this wears off, not like you did. I don't think I have the strength." Cass shakes her head. "I can still feel her. In my body. In my blood. It's only—" she glances at me with that same odd expression, then away again. "It's only what you gave me that's put a barrier up. And I don't know how long it will last."

Connor gets in between Cass and Antoine then, growling at Antoine until he backs off, his hands held up. My brother the wolf looks up at Cass, and she must see something in his eyes the rest of us don't, for she cries out in a low voice, and then, when he turns and runs swiftly and silently from the clearing, she follows, and the two disappear into the darkness.

The wolves follow them, and when Remy pauses at the edge of the clearing and looks back, Lori takes Avery by the hand. "They may still need us," she says. "We have to follow them."

"Jeremiah," Antoine says. "Go with Tate. He'll keep you safe. I'll take care of Harper."

For a moment Jeremiah looks like he might argue. Then he looks at my face, and whatever he sees there makes up his mind. "It's your funeral," he mutters, then turns and follows Tate from the clearing.

Then Antoine's arms are around me, his mouth on mine bruising and hot. I can feel the tension in his body, and I know that he was as afraid for me as I was for him. "I'm sorry," he murmurs against my lips. "I never should have left you." He tips my head back, his hands cradling my face. "I was so damned scared when I saw you there."

"I thought I was going to lose you." My voice shakes. "I could feel her, the power she has over you."

"Keziah's power over me is gone. If she didn't know it before, she does now." Antoine holds my face in his hands, his eyes blazing in a way that rearranges the particles of my body.

"For how long?"

"For now, at least." His voice trembles slightly and one thumb brushes the tension of my jaw. "It's you who holds the power now."

"Do I?" My voice is barely audible. I know what I'm really asking, but I can't find the words.

Antoine is so close it's hard to breathe. "If I start with you," he says roughly, "I know I won't stop. Do you understand me, Harper? I won't be able to stop." He holds my face. "Not anymore."

I take one more step, breaking the last distance between us.

"Then don't," I whisper.

He pulls me against the hard length of him, his eyes searching mine. "Are you sure? Are you truly sure, Harper?"

I know what he is asking. I know it isn't about a piece of paper, or the binding, or even about the physical act of love itself. He's asking me something else, something that goes beyond life and time, a question I know he has always felt he has no right to ask.

"Always." I raise my hand and thread it through his, so the emerald gleams beside his silver band in the moonlight. "Always," I say again.

He groans, and his mouth lands on mine. "Then I'm taking you home."

He gathers me into his arms as if I weigh no more than a leaf, and a moment later, we're speeding through the night, towards the Marigny mansion that is ours.

CHAPTER 17

JASMINE

I wake in the predawn to the sensual touch of night jasmine trailing through the open window. I turn toward it with my eyes closed still. The day is yet to break, I can tell by the softness behind my closed lids, and I wonder for a moment if the predawn damp is why the jasmine seems touched by cedar and cypress, a woody note. Then I feel a light trail up the bare skin of my thigh to my hip, sending shockwaves of sensation through my body, and the events of last night reassert themselves in my mind. I freeze, the languorous trail of Antoine's fingers up over my hip pinning me in place. His lips press against the soft skin under my ear, and I can tell he is smiling.

"You should go back to sleep." His lips trace fire down the nape of my neck and farther, along my spine. One large hand cradles my hip as I arch toward him, and he laughs softly against my back. "If you keep moving like that, I will never leave this bed."

. . .

THE SUN IS HIGH IN THE SKY WHEN I WAKE AGAIN, THIS TIME deeply refreshed, as if my body has been utterly rearranged and reborn. I stretch across the bed, only to freeze when I realize it is empty. My eyelids fly open. The four-poster is in complete disarray, pillows flung about the room, fairy lights hanging at odd angles, the sheets so tangled and wild I flush just looking at them. Every image offers another memory that makes my body melt and my skin turn to fire.

I hear the faint clatter of crockery below with a surge of relief. Antoine hasn't left, then. I brush my teeth hastily, grab a sheet, and pad downstairs, pausing at the kitchen door.

Antoine is leaning against one of the columns on the porch, nursing a cup of coffee. In the moment before he turns around, I catch a glimpse of his face in profile and feel a twist of worry at the dark, hooded expression I see there. A moment later I'm sure I must have been mistaken, for when he turns to me, gold gleams in the cobalt blue, and he pulls me into him and kisses me so thoroughly I'm ready to drop the sheet when he is done.

"You should always wear your hair like that." He tugs at a piece hanging by my waist. "You look like a mermaid straight from the sea."

"It will take me a week to comb it out." I'm about to add, after last night, but at the memory of how my hair ended up so liberated, my face flames so bright that I temporarily lose my powers of speech. A slow, wicked grin lifts Antoine's mouth, and I'm so distracted by it that when he speaks again I have to force myself to focus.

"I said, perhaps you'd better find something other than a sheet to wear. You'll be late for school."

"School?" I try to ignore the slow, maddening trail of his hand as it moves from my waist up to the bare skin above the sheet.

"You know." He pulls me close, so my arms go around his

neck and his nearness is the only thing keeping the sheet up. "That place you go to learn."

"I think," I whisper, as bends my head to the side and tracks my neck with his mouth, "that I'd rather stay here and learn."

"And I think," he murmurs against my skin, "if we do this for one moment more, that sheet will be more torn than it already is."

My mouth curls in a slow, secret smile. "Is that right." I kiss him, hard, and then with a speed to rival his on a good day, I step back and let the sheet fall.

"Christ, Harper."

I have the satisfaction of seeing his eyes darken and narrow, his body go taut and still. His eyes roam over my naked body, so slowly I feel as if they burn where they touch. By the time they reach my own, the gold flecks are gone, and there is nothing but the hard slate of desire. Then his hands lift me and my legs wrap around his waist, rough denim against the soft skin of my inner thighs, the heat of him pressing against me. My arms twine around his neck, his mouth hot and hungry on mine as he carries me up the stairs.

I guess school will have to wait.

It's late afternoon, the moonflowers sleeping in the sunlight. I'm lying across Antoine's chest, his hand playing idly through my hair. I can feel the rise and fall of his body under my own.

"Do vampires actually have to breathe?" I ask.

Hi chest rumbles with laughter beneath my cheek. "Strictly speaking, no. It's one of those strange things, though. I guess our bodies automatically do what they did when they were alive. I don't need oxygen to live, but it feels—uncomfortable — to cease breathing. Even though I know it can't kill me, I still dislike the feeling."

"I can't imagine what it would be like to not need breath."

His hand stills in my hair. "I hope you never find out." I hear the change in his voice and wince inside. In a swift movement he is up and out of the bed. I prop myself up on one elbow, unable to stop myself admiring the extraordinary, savage sculpture of him, the way it seems as if the sun lights him from within, making his skin glow bronze over the long, corded muscle. I ache to touch every part of him all over again, even as he disappears into the bathroom. When he emerges he is hidden by a towel, shaking water from his hair as he rakes his fingers through it.

"I need to find your brother," he says, his back turned to me as he pulls on his jeans. There's something careful in his voice, and my eyes narrow.

"What aren't you telling me?"

"Nothing." He gives me a sideways smile that I find in no way reassuring. "I should have gone after them this morning, but—" he raises his eyebrows as he buttons his shirt "—I got distracted."

"Well, I'm not going to let you distract me." I wrap the sheet tightly around me and fold my arms over it. "What's going on?"

He gives me a wry smile. "To start with, I don't know where your brother and Cass are. I don't know what happened to them, or where Keziah and Caleb went. I haven't heard from Tate." He glances at his phone and gives me a small smile. "Although that might be because I switched my phone off somewhere around midnight."

I try not to color.

"But I do need to find them," he goes on. "And you need to eat something."

"When will you come back?" I try not to sound too eager.

"When I know what's happened." He moves to the bed so swiftly I don't realize it until he is leaning over me, his mouth touching mine. He is gone just as fast, standing in the doorway, smiling at me ruefully. "I can't stay," he says. "I won't leave if I do."

I feel suddenly bereft.

Then I remember something, and although it seems completely stupid and juvenile in the current circumstances, I ask it anyway, because something inside me needs to know that there is another chapter, that our story doesn't end here, in golden sunlight and the coming dusk.

"Do you remember me telling you about the Midwinter Ball?"

"This is what's on your mind right now?" Antoine looks at me quizzically.

"Not really." I flush, but I'm determined to go on, no matter how silly it might seem to him. "It's on this Saturday night. Now that Cass is safe, and . . . well, everything, I wanted to ask you again if you would go with me."

"I really don't think it's a good idea." His smile has gone, replaced by the somewhat grim expression from earlier, on the porch.

My stomach twists in disappointment. I turn my head away so he can't see my face, and nod quietly. "I understand."

I'm aware of him still and silent in the doorway. When I glance back his eyes are hooded, but his mouth twists in a reluctant smile.

"You do realize how unfair it is to ask me questions when you are wrapped in a sheet, with your hair out and wild?"

I look at him, my heart lifting. "Does that mean you'll come?"

He shakes his head ruefully. "As if I can say no."

When I make to leap from the bed, he holds up a restraining hand and backs out onto the landing, his eyes both darkening and laughing at me. "Don't even think about it, Harper Marigny. I have things to do and places to go, and neither of those things are going to happen if you drop that sheet again."

The sun streams golden through the window, catching us

both where we're suddenly frozen, staring at one another, making his eyes blaze.

"What did you just call me?" I whisper.

A shadow chases over his face, and it goes by turn from grim to blazing then back to something else, something I haven't seen before, don't recognize, and don't know what to make of. "You heard me," he says. His eyes travel to the emerald on my finger then back up to my face.

"It really is always now, isn't it," I say quietly, holding his eyes.

He nods. "Yes," he says. "Yes, Harper. It is."

Then he is gone, and I am left wondering if *always* is what Antoine truly wants, or if it is simply what he has committed to.

CHAPTER 18

SILK

I'm not certain what I expect to happen after the night we spent together, but Antoine disappearing for the next three days sure isn't it.

"Remy's gone, too," says Avery gloomily. It's Friday, and we're in Deepwater, shopping for dresses. The selection isn't huge, but neither of us feels inclined to drive all the way to Jackson. I'm beginning to wonder if there's any point buying a dress at all. I haven't heard from Connor, Cass, or Tate, and despite a few short text messages, Antoine has been completely absent. I want to believe it has nothing to do with how he feels about me, or what has happened between us, but the doubts creep in regardless. In three days, I've gone from euphoric to imagining the worst possible scenarios, including Antoine disappearing permanently. I've channeled my fears into painting. The mural in the library is almost finished. It's more soothing than the night garden, which has become so linked in my mind to Antoine that being in it is unbearable right now.

"Remy hasn't called, then?"

Avery shakes her head. "Lori told me not to worry, but it

isn't that simple. It wasn't only Connor who bit Caleb. Henri got him, too."

I remember Henri. He's Remy's brother.

"Which means," Avery continues, "that Keziah will be hunting for Henri as well as Connor, since only the blood of the wolves that bit Caleb can cure him. Remy told me they were going to run. I just didn't think it would be far—or for long."

"I guess phones aren't really a thing for wolves," I say doubtfully. We look at one another, and suddenly we're laughing aloud. After the long days of tension, laughter feels good. "It's all so crazy," I whisper, wiping my eyes. The shop assistant is looking at us suspiciously, which sends us off into another fit of giggles. "Here we are, shopping for dresses like any other normal teenagers, trying to work out how a werewolf might use a cellphone."

"I'm starting to find it hard to live both of those lives." Avery's laughter dies as fast as it came. "I'm lying to my parents, my friends, everyone." She meets my eyes. "And Cass's mom," she says quietly. "I've known Selena for as long as I can remember, Harper. Every time she tells me how happy she is that Cass is coming and going from her studies in Biloxi, I want to cry and scream at the same time. I don't know how this story ends for them, Harper. I don't even know what Cass herself wants."

"I miss Cass." I touch a rose silk dress absently. "And I miss my brother."

"I know." Avery touches a green dress with the same lack of attention. "I miss them, too."

"Ladies," says the shop assistant frostily. "Are we buying, or are we gossiping?"

We look at one another and burst into another fit of giggles, and it feels better than good to have a friend again.

. . .

On Saturday, Avery and I agree she will come to the mansion so we can get ready together. Neither of us has heard anything from Antoine or Remy.

"We may be escorting each other to this ball," says Avery, eying her green dress doubtfully. "And I'm not sure what I was thinking when I bought this."

"It's beautiful," I say, and it is. "Not that it matters, Avery. You could wear a burlap sack and still be the most stunning girl in the room." It's true. Cass, in her immortal perfection, may be dramatic, but Avery, with her flawless skin, high cheekbones, slanted eyes and long limbs, is so beautiful I sometimes find myself gazing at her as one would a painting in a gallery, just admiring the view.

"Pity Remy doesn't seem to think so." She gives me a rueful smile. "But just look at us, moping about here. We don't need men to make this ball a party. We're going to dress up, and look beautiful, and if my wolf and your vampire stand us both up, then too bad, right?"

"Right." I nod determinedly.

"We're definitely going to need champagne." Avery reaches into her bag and waves a bottle triumphantly in the air. "Left over from my party." Our eyes meet. "Okay," she grimaces. "Maybe not the best memory. But you have to admit I had good wine."

"You definitely did have good wine."

She pops the cork and fills our glasses. "To friends."

"To friends." We clink glasses and drink. Avery puts on some great tunes, and for the next couple of hours, we're just two girls getting a little illegal buzz on before a ball.

"So," Avery says, wielding curling tongs with dexterity through her long hair, "I take it you and vamp boy have finally . . . ?"

I flush.

"Oh, I know that look. You so have." She grins wickedly at me in the mirror. "So?"

"So what?" I drop my eyes and busy myself with hairpins.

"Don't give me that." Avery rolls her eyes. "How was it?"

"It was—amazing." Even saying that much brings back a flood of memories: of Antoine following the pale moonlight along my body, the heat of his mouth, the light of a thousand stars behind my eyes.

"Oh, wow." I realize Avery is staring at me in the mirror. "That good, huh?"

My flushed face turns to a blazing inferno. "Well, I thought so." I toy with a hairbrush. "But it can't have been that good, if he's able to just walk away."

"Harper." Avery swivels on the stool and pins me with a knowing eye. "In some things you are definitely much smarter than me. That garden of yours, your art; sometimes you seem so much older, somehow, more mature than the rest of us, that I forget there are some things that you know nothing about at all. Like men, for example."

"What are you trying to say?"

"Has it occurred to you that the reason Antoine has run so far, so fast, is because it was so good between you, rather than because it wasn't?"

I stare at her in bewilderment. "But that makes absolutely no sense."

"Oh, yes it does." Avery turns back to the mirror and sticks pins in her hair with alarming efficiency. "And I'll offer you another piece of Avery Fairweather wisdom: no matter how far he runs, vamp boy won't be able to stay away." She shakes the hairbrush at me. "You can bank on that."

I shake my head, laughing despite myself.

The day is fading, the bottle gone, and Avery and I not just a little tipsy, when the sound of a truck in the drive makes us both freeze.

"Do I dare think we may just have dates after all?" Avery and I stare at each other. My heart is racing. It seems a little pathetic to feel so nervous. But I can't help throwing myself a critical look in the mirror, wondering if I should have left my hair down instead of piling it into a mountain of curls, or if the rose silk isn't cut just a little too low in the front.

"You look perfect," says Avery, winking at me.

One car door slams.

We tense.

Then another.

"Two humans," murmurs Avery. We catch one another's eye. "Okay, not quite humans," she says, and we go off into another fit of nervous giggles.

"Well? Are you coming down, or are we coming up?"

My heart trips at the sound of Antoine's voice floating up the stairs, low and rich and so full of humor I feel a wave of reassurance sweep over me.

"That's our cue." I put out my arm to Avery and we emerge from the room to stand at the top of the stairs.

"I feel like Scarlett O'Hara," mutters Avery, but the nerves in her voice mirror my own. Then the two figures below turn to look up at us, and suddenly I don't feel nervous at all, just swept away.

Antoine and Remy are clad in tuxedos, but they wear them with a careless elegance that I know will make every other man in the room seem poorly dressed. Perhaps it is their innate physicality, the undeniability of their supernatural forms, that turns the stiff formal dress into something fluid and graceful. Whatever it is, when I look down and see the way Antoine leans laconically against the doorframe, hands thrust in his pockets, hair disheveled and yet somehow perfect, his tanned skin glowing above the crisp white shirt, I feel something in me go weak. His eyes narrow and darken as I move downstairs, traveling over the rose silk as if it weren't there. The thought reminds me that he knows very well what lies beneath my dress, has in fact owned every quivering inch, and that in turn turns my insides to liquid and my skin to fire. As I reach the wide final step, I'm vaguely aware of Remy and Avery murmuring off to my right, but all I can really focus on is Antoine's nearness, and the way he is looking at me.

"I wasn't sure you'd be here," I say.

His hands rest on my hips and lift me lightly from the last step to the floor then pull me against him. "I said I would be here." His eyes roam downward, then back to my face. One large hand frames my face. "I wouldn't have missed seeing you like this." He is no longer smiling. "You're stunning, Harper."

I laugh awkwardly and look away. He turns my face back so his eyes find mine. "Stunning," he says again, quietly.

I sway toward him, but at the last moment, he pulls away, smiling crookedly. "I don't think that's wise," he murmurs, "if we plan to get to that ball any time tonight."

"Are we going, or am I drinking rum on your back porch?" Remy grins at us, Avery curled into him like a cat against a sun-warmed wall.

"Going," I say mechanically, trying to ignore Antoine's thumb stroking the bare skin on my back with maddening slowness. "Definitely going."

"Then let's do this," Remy says.

We step out of the mansion into the night, on our way to the ball.

CHAPTER 19

BALL

The Midwinter Ball is held at the Baudelaire Plantation, one of the original antebellum mansions in Deepwater Hollow, still owned by the Baudelaire family. We're met at the door by Jared, who looks stiff and uncomfortable in his formal attire as he greets his parent's guests—a discomfort made little better when he is confronted by Antoine and Remy's effortless elegance.

"Is Cass coming?" he greets Avery and I, barely nodding at the men on either side of us.

"I'm not really sure." I hope my voice sounds steady.

"I hope so. This night needs something to liven it up." He lowers his voice as he leans in. "I've got some weed upstairs, if you guys want to come up later."

"Maybe later," Avery says, rolling her eyes at me behind his back as we pass him and enter.

"Wow," I say as we enter the formal ballroom, and Avery and Remy wander off to talk to some people from school. "Now I really do feel as if I'm reliving Gone with the Wind."

"They've barely changed a thing." Antoine looks around with distaste. "The only difference is that the slaves are paid, now."

He looks pointedly at the servants moving between the guests with trays of champagne.

"You've been here before?"

"The Baudelaire family was here when my family built the Marigny mansion," Antoine says. "They were one of the original families. French colonists, just as my family were. They had the same pretensions. And the same prejudices." His mouth twists in contempt as he looks around at the gold leaf on the cornices and tall paintings on the walls, which inevitably depict noble-looking ancestors and peaceful pastoral scenes. "And it seems they are just as given to whitewashing history as the rest of the South."

"I can't imagine how it must be," I say, as he stops a passing waiter and gets us both a glass of champagne. "To revisit a place like this after so long."

"The last time I was here was the Midwinter Ball of 1865—right before war broke out." He smiles wryly as I try to process this. "I'd heard that Marie, a Marigny daughter, was engaged to a Baudelaire. I came back to remind Marie of the need to retain her own name, since the men of the family, I suspected, would soon be heading off to be blown up on a field somewhere."

"And did she listen?" I ask, intrigued.

His smile fades. "I'm afraid I didn't give her much choice."

"Did she marry the man she was engaged to?"

"Unfortunately, his family wasn't so happy about their new daughter-in-law bucking southern traditions by doing something so outlandish as retaining her own name. She begged me to reconsider. I didn't, I'm afraid. As it turns out, the gentleman in question didn't survive his first battle, so it was irrelevant in the end, not that Marie ever saw it that way." He turns the champagne glass in his hands and meets my eyes. "You said once that you didn't believe the stories of the terrible things I've done. I told you that at some time, they have all been true. I meant it, Harper. I wasn't always so reluctant to compel people.

Nor did I hesitate to do what had to be done to guard the binding on the mansion. No matter who it affected."

"But you aren't like that anymore." Even I can hear the uncertainty in my voice.

"I was." He steps forward and wraps one of my curls around his finger. "Until I met you."

The ballroom drops away, so there is only him and me and the dark longing in his eyes. "Where were you?" I whisper. "You were gone. For days."

"Searching for Keziah."

"Did you find her?"

He shakes his head slowly.

"I thought you weren't coming back."

Instead of answering, he steps closer. "Dance with me," he says roughly. He takes the glass from my hand and puts it on the sideboard, and I have no thought of refusing.

Antoine leads me onto the floor. The room is full of the dignitaries and old families who form what passes as aristocracy in Deepwater. Normally I would be rigid with tension and nerves. Despite Connor's name on the Legacy Grant, these aren't my people, or an environment in which I feel comfortable. But Antoine's tall assurance seems to lend us both a certain presence, and I'm aware of the hard-eyed, blond matrons watching us with reluctant approval as Antoine moves me effortlessly across the floor.

I've never taken dancing lessons. Even the thought of doing such a thing is laughable. Yet in Antoine's arms, the movements seem easy, something I don't need to think of, and I realize with a faint shock that I'm actually enjoying myself.

"What is it?" Antoine murmurs against my ear. "I can feel you smiling." He spins me beneath his arm and draws me back in, his hand warm and exciting on my back.

"I like this," I say, looking up at him. "I like dancing with you like this." He gives me the slow smile that always makes my knees weak and draws me against him, moving our bodies so it seems they are one.

"They're all looking at you," I say, catching a glimpse of the curious faces as he spins me again.

"No, Harper." He brings me back against him. "They're all looking at you."

I'm still smiling at that when a high, cold voice interrupts us.

"Perhaps, Antoine, they may have been looking at your little human a moment ago. Now, however, they are all looking at me."

In an abrupt movement, Antoine spins me around so I am behind him, maneuvering us both off the dance floor, watching Keziah warily. She is standing alone amid the dancers, clad in a crimson silk sheath that makes the men in the room stare unabashedly and their wives purse their lips disapprovingly. With a small, knowing smile curving her lips, she sashays off the dance floor toward us, clearly aware that she holds every eye in the room. A barrel-chested man in his fifties whom I recognize as a town council member hands her a glass of champagne as she passes and is rewarded with a seductive smile that leaves him staring after her in a dazed fashion. She appears before us, and I realize Remy has materialized to stand at Antoine's side. Then, with a jolt of both relief and trepidation, I see Tate, tuxedo-clad and quietly, devastatingly handsome, standing on Antoine's other side.

"Brother," Tate says quietly, "the wolves are outside, in the field beyond the mansion."

Antoine nods, then glares at Keziah. "What do you want here?"

I'm amazed that the ball is continuing around us, the entire room oblivious to the fact that a group of ruthless killers stand in their midst, bloody carnage only moments away.

Keziah nods in my direction without looking at me. "I want

her brother and the other wolf to cure Caleb. And I want my child back where she belongs—at my side."

"Caleb is not yet dead?" Antoine frowns. "We tried to track you for days. I found no trace of him."

Keziah's mouth curls. "You, of all people, should know you cannot track me, Antoine. Not unless I summon you." Her hand darts out to cup Antoine's face, and her eyes narrow. "Although perhaps that may change," she murmurs, her eyes sliding sideways to me. "Now that you've taken the girl after all." She steps back and regards him with an almost admiring expression. "I confess, I had not thought you still so ruthless, child of mine. I am impressed."

"You need to leave." Antoine's voice is cold and hard. "You have no place here, in this room."

"Oh, I disagree." Keziah sips her champagne, eying Antoine seductively over the rim of her glass. "This room is my chessboard. The people in it are pawns. And unless you do as I ask, each one of them will be sacrificed without mercy until the game is mine." Her eyes travel across the room to settle on Selena, who is animatedly talking with a friend in the corner. "I plan to start with her," Keziah says musingly. "Cass's mother. She has become tediously difficult to compel—and I fear she holds Cass back from her full potential."

"You will not touch her." Antoine's voice is lethal.

"So forceful." Keziah smiles at him. "I always liked you that way, Antoine. Ruthless. Merciless. Those are your finest qualities, you know." She looks me up and down again with detached interest. "Taking the girl means you are finally reclaiming your true nature, Antoine. I'm glad. But do tell me. Why is it you have yet to give her your blood?"

Antoine tenses. Violence hangs in the air, dangerously close to eruption, when Tate speaks. "Antoine." He nods at the door. "Look."

As we turn around, Selena gasps, and a murmur of excitement goes through the crowd.

Standing in the doorway hand in hand, so beautiful, savage, and wild they seem almost to belong to a different universe, are Connor and Cass.

The man in the doorway is the brother I have always known. He is also something else entirely, something I have never known.

Connor is usually found in the back of any room. In company such as this, he would be uncomfortable in his formal attire, loosening his tie at the first opportunity and seeking an escape to the back of the mansion, where he'd most likely spend the night drinking beer with the busboys, possibly fixing something that had broken in the kitchen.

But this Connor is taller. Stronger. And utterly self-assured.

From the doorway, he regards the crowd with detached amusement. He looks as effortlessly elegant in his perfectly fitting tuxedo as his wolf brother and the two vampires on either side of me. His hand rests confidently on the small of Cass's back, and when she turns to whisper something in his ear, his mouth curls into a slow smile I've never seen on his face.

I'm the only one focused on Connor, though.

Cass's white silk dress is entirely backless, cut so daringly low the peak of the V rests at the very top of the perfect swell of her buttocks. She is clearly naked beneath the dress. She regards the crowd with the same slight amusement as Connor, as if they share a private joke which nobody else is part of. They enter the ballroom seeming entirely unconcerned that they have captured the full attention of every person in attendance—and just as oblivious to the stunned expression on Cass's mother's face.

"I'm going to Selena," Avery hisses in my ear. I nod wordlessly as she pushes through the crowd to where Selena is staring at Cass, as if seeing her daughter for the first time.

"Oh," murmurs Keziah slyly. "I forgot to mention that I

removed the compulsion that hid Cass from her mother's eyes and made Selena believe Cass was unchanged. Now she sees her daughter as Cass truly is, her new form. Selena is wondering what, exactly, her daughter is."

"You can't play with people like that," I say, too angry to be careful.

Keziah raises her eyebrows at me. "I can do whatever I want," she says coldly. "I've been doing whatever I want for longer than you can begin to imagine. Don't get in my way, little girl. And if you interfere with my plans again, you will die—be sure of it."

"And if you take so much as one step closer to her," says Antoine, his eyes glittering with gold fury, "it is your existence that will end."

"I'd love to see you attempt it, Antoine. I truly would." Keziah smiles, but there is no humor in her face now. "I meant what I said. Unless you wish to see this monstrosity of a ballroom covered in blood, give me the wolves to cure Caleb and give me Cass." She looks around in distaste. "I assure you there is little I would like more than to see these smug fools scream for their lives as I drain every one of them."

"But you won't do that, Keziah."

It's Connor who speaks. I'm so taken aback I can only stare. This can't be my brother, this hard-eyed man with one hand thrust in his pocket, lounging against the sideboard with lethal stillness, looking every bit as dangerous—and more—as Antoine, Tate, or Remy. The latter, I notice, comes to Connor's side as if it's my brother who commands him, rather than Remy himself being the leader of the pack. Connor seems to accept Remy's presence at his side unquestioningly. His free hand still rests loosely on Cass's back, and she, too, eyes Keziah with a fierce independence I can't begin to understand. She has yet to so much as look at Selena, her own mother.

"Oh?" Keziah raises one perfectly arched eyebrow disdainfully. "A wolf less than a week, and already so confident you dare challenge me?"

"But I'm not just a wolf." Connor holds her eyes, smiling faintly. "As you well know, Keziah, since the reason you can't challenge me is also the reason Caleb never recovered from his bite. You didn't understand that when it happened, did you? A wolf bite has never been something for you to fear, at least not before. But now you know that nothing here can help you. You know it's too late."

"Oh?" Keziah's tone is low and menacing. Her smile fades, and her eyes flash dangerously. "And why is that?"

"Because Caleb is dead." It's Cass who answers this time, staring at Keziah with a small, hard smile that sends chills down my spine. Keziah hisses with fury, her eyes a sick red. "I felt it," Cass says coldly. "And then I tracked you both to the place where his body lays and made sure of it myself. No wolf blood can help him now—not that it ever really could have. And as for me—well." She takes a step closer to Keziah, and for the first time I see a faint crack in my brother's confident expression. But he does nothing to stop Cass. It's only because I know him that I see the hard line of his lips, the faint narrowing of his eyes as Cass comes within touching distance of her Maker. "Why don't you try to summon me?" Cass whispers. "Caleb is dead now. Gone from this world forever. You know it's true; you must have felt it, even if you were busy running after the wolves and didn't want to believe it. That was our doing, too, laying a thousand scents to throw you off our tracks. You wasted all that time playing games. Now it's too late. Caleb is gone, and you are alone, Keziah. So, please—try. Try to summon me." Cass's eyes glow briefly with a fiery, savage light. Selena gasps again, and I realize Cass's mother is barely steps away from Keziah now, coming toward her daughter, staring at Cass in shock and confusion.

Keziah's hands clench into fists. She stares hard at Cass. I feel the faint thud on the air, the ripple I felt back in the clearing when Keziah called both Cass and Antoine. Antoine shudders beside me. Cass rocks on her feet slightly, then regains her balance and stares back at Keziah defiantly, the small smile on her face again.

"You can't do it." Cass smiles coldly at her Maker. "You can't summon me. Not anymore."

Keziah is staring at her, eyes wide and furious, colors shifting across them in an unnatural rainbow that I hope nobody else in the room is seeing. The facade of humanity has fallen away, her anger revealing the supernatural creature beneath, in the stark tension of her form, the strange colors in her eyes, and her preternatural stillness, like a wild animal coiled to strike. I tense, bracing myself for the attack I am suddenly certain is coming.

"Cass?" Selena's uncertain voice cuts across the tension. Cass's mother is standing beside Keziah, but Selena has eyes only for the creature who used to be her daughter, her face dazed as she takes in the strange apparition before her. "Cass, what's happened to you? What's going on?"

"Mom—" Cass begins to speak, but her voice breaks. She curls into Connor's side and my brother's arm pulls her close protectively. Shadows chase over her face, the different layers that make up Cass seeming to emerge and retreat. At one moment she is the gentle girl her mother raised. In the next, her eyes flash with the savagery of her malevolent Maker. Then Cass draws a deep breath, and Noya's sad wisdom softens her face. She opens her mouth, and I think she is going to say something that will help, or at least compel the terrible confusion from her mother's face, when Keziah seizes Selena with lethal swiftness.

Sinking her teeth into Selena's neck, Keziah tears out her throat with one fierce, furious snarl. When she finally releases her, Selena slumps to the floor, wide-eyed and utterly, finally dead.

Keziah throws back her head and shrieks. Blood streams down her face as the unearthly cry dies in her throat. With one last, savage look of triumph at Cass, Keziah is gone from the ballroom, leaving Selena's lifeless form bleeding out on the floor, and the crowd of ball goers staring at each other in horror.

CHAPTER 20

DESTINY

The next hour is a blur.

Antoine, Cass, and Tate compel the entire gathering—no small feat, given that there are two hundred guests plus the serving staff. Remy and the wolves take Selena's body away. "All you remember is that she suffered a fatal heart attack," I hear Antoine murmur over and again. "Yes, a terrible tragedy, but nothing more."

That story requires more compulsion, this time with the coroner and the mortuary. By the early hours of the morning, Selena's body, overseen by Tate and Antoine, is being prepared for burial with a rapidity that would be unthinkable in normal circumstances, and Cass is sitting in my kitchen with Avery and me, silent and still. My brother is off somewhere with Remy. He hasn't told me where he is going. I didn't ask. I don't feel like I have that right, anymore. I don't know who this new Connor is, but I do know he no longer belongs to me in the way he once did.

He belongs to Cass.

"I love him," she says now. She sits upright on one of the old wooden chairs in our kitchen, uncannily still and straight, her wild eyes strange and unsettling. "The way I feel about Connor is the one thing I am certain of. Even tonight—my mother—I didn't feel it. Not really."

Avery and I don't look at each other, but I'm certain she is as taken aback as I am.

Cass smiles faintly. "You're shocked." She nods. "I understand that. I remember how it was, being human. And I do remember how much I loved my mother. I just can't feel it anymore, if that makes sense. I know I loved her, that once she was the person I cared about most in the world. But since Keziah made me, since I became what I am, it's as if everything I felt back then is gone. Parts of me are still there, inside me. They're just different parts, and they cling to different things."

"What do you mean by that?" Despite my shock, I'm genuinely curious.

Cass turns the unsettling eyes to me. They seem to shimmer with light, like Keziah's. It's odd, like an oil slick on water, iridescent and unnatural. "Of course you want to know." She nods. "You wonder what Antoine was like before he became what he is. What's left of the man he was. I know, though. I could tell you." I don't like the strange light in her eyes when she says it. "Because of Keziah, I can see Antoine as he once was. Before he was made. The man he used to be. Because Keziah made us both, I'm connected to Antoine forever, in a way you can't begin to understand."

"Then tell me." I'm unable to keep the edge from my voice.

"No," she says simply. "It isn't my story. But I will say that there is a lot he should tell you, Harper. Things you should know. You don't have any idea what is truly going on with you. Why Antoine is with you. What you are."

"Antoine is with Harper because he loves her," says Avery sharply. "And the Cass I used to know would never have said something so cruel."

Cass raises her eyebrows. "I told you," she says. "I'm no longer that person."

"Then tell us who you are now," I say, trying to forget what she just said about Antoine. "You said you love Connor. Is it the same as before you turned—or different?"

"Both." Cass looks over my shoulder, and I realize she is trying to think of how to explain. "I barely know myself," she says. "I have Noya inside me, this strong, fierce presence." She shakes her head. "I never knew how strong she was," she says wonderingly. "She seemed so gentle. But she is fierce, and wild. She knows things. Things I don't know if she was even aware of, when she lived."

Avery nods. "That's true," she says quietly. "She talks to me, too."

"Then you understand." Cass nods. "Noya is within me, and if I look in the mirror, I see her, perhaps even more than I see myself. I realized that the Cass I used to be wasn't truly shy and gentle. She was just scared. Noya has taken that girl and created something harder—stronger—from her. Noya and Cass are like one person inside me, but a new one, one I don't really know yet."

It's strange to hear Cass speak of herself in the third person, but fascinating, too. "And then there's Keziah." Cass shakes her head. "She's inside me too, seductive and powerful. Part of her is calling me, and part of her *is* me. When she calls, I can't tell if the voice comes from within, or without."

"And Connor?" I press her, wanting to understand my brother through her eyes, to know some of what they are to one another.

"The part of me who is Cass," she says slowly, "the old Cass, the girl I was once, is tied to Connor. He holds me in his blood. I felt it when his teeth closed on my neck, and again when he gave me his blood to stop the wolf poison from spreading. It's as if something in his blood anchors me, holds the last shred of my humanity. It was the only thing that was strong enough to overcome Keziah." She looks at me. "It wasn't your blood that did that, Harper," she says with an odd hostility. "Not whatever it is running through your veins that has Antoine so bound to your side he barely knows himself anymore."

I frown. "What?"

"Cass." Avery glances at me. "None of this is Harper's fault. This isn't fair."

"Isn't it?" Cass's eyes are glowing again, not in a friendly way. "You think that all you like, Avery. But the truth is that everything that's happened here in Deepwater has happened because of her." She stares at me coldly. "Even Caleb's death is because of Harper. And yet you," she sneers, "don't even understand what you are."

Every one of her words hammers home, hurts in a way I hadn't imagined possible. I want to ask what she means, but something tells me it's the wrong way to find out. And, although I'm ashamed to admit it, something else just doesn't want to give her the satisfaction.

"Connor," I force myself to say. "You were talking about my brother."

"Yes." The hostility fades from Cass's eyes, and I release a breath I hadn't realized I was holding. "Loving Connor is the only emotion I know now. Loving Connor, wanting him. I want him so much. All the time, Harper. More even than blood." Her voice is distracted, and she doesn't seem to be aware of how odd the conversation is.

"We get it," Avery says hastily, casting me a worried look. "You can't keep your hands off wolf boy."

"It's more than that." Cass meets her eyes. "We're linked," she says simply. "Forever. I'm inside him, and he's inside me. We belong together. We won't ever belong to anyone else. Only to each other."

"What about the mansion?" I hear the pathetic, pleading note in my voice. "Will he just walk away from that now, too? From everything we've worked toward?"

"I don't know." She speaks as if it's the first time she's thought of it. "We haven't talked about it." Her eyes shift to Avery. "You know Connor leads the pack now. The wolves aren't Remy's anymore."

"Yes," says Avery quietly. "Remy told me."

"Do you know why?"

Avery's eyes flicker to me. "I have an idea."

I'm getting really tired of everyone seeming to know things I don't.

Cass stiffens, her eyes moving rapidly as she seems to listen to something we can't hear. "Connor is back." Abruptly she is out of her seat and gone, too fast for me to register her movements.

"Weird." Avery glances at me, her concern visible. "That was so weird. Are you okay, Harper? Cass said some harsh things. I'm sure she doesn't mean them. It's just the vampire stuff, I guess."

"Oh, she meant them." I stand up. "Now I just need to find out if Connor feels the same way."

"Harper—" Avery stands up and puts out a hand as if to stop me, but I shake my head and keep walking. I'm tired of hiding from it all. If my brother intends to leave his project—and me—behind, I'd rather know about it now.

When I come out onto the porch, Connor is kissing Cass by his truck, her arms entwined about him and his enclosing her so profoundly it's hard to see where one leaves off and the other begins. It's such an intimate embrace I turn to walk back inside, hoping they didn't hear me, but that would be ignoring vamp hearing and whatever heightened senses my brother now possesses. They pull apart, Cass looking at me with open hostility, my brother with a guarded expression.

"I'm sorry," I mutter. "It's a bad time."

"No." Connor's voice is deeper, more self-assured than before. "I came to talk to you, Harper." He touches Cass's face. "Wait for me at the cabin?"

Cass nods, casting me a resentful look. She kisses Connor again, deeply enough to make me look away uncomfortably. She is gone with uncanny speed, leaving Connor and me staring at each other. Avery slips out the door behind me. "I'll talk to you later, Harper. Hey, Connor."

"Hey." My brother has always been slightly wary of Avery, scooting out of her path when possible, mumbling incoherent responses the rest of the time. Not anymore. He meets her eyes confidently, nods coolly as he returns her greeting. When she passes close by him on the way to her car, he doesn't flinch, though he doesn't exactly smile, either. There is something lethal in his stillness as he leans against his truck. My brother has become darker.

I wait until Avery's car has disappeared until I speak. "Beer?" I go to the cooler.

"Sure." He doesn't move, though, just leans against his truck and looks up at the mansion, as if he's never really seen it before. I pass him a beer and open one for myself, then sit on the porch steps. The night is dark, stars pinpricks in the sky above. The magnolia tree, I notice, seems to have fewer flowers on it than before. For some odd reason this makes me happy. Maybe the trees will shed their flowers, I think, and go back to being normal.

Maybe I will, too.

"Do you remember when I first showed you this place?" It's an odd question. Connor still isn't looking at me, but at the mansion behind me.

"Sure," I say. "You drove me up here from Baton Rouge. We had a picnic under the red magnolia, and you told me all about your plans."

"No." Connor takes a long pull on his beer. He still doesn't look at me. "Before that. The day I first showed you a picture of it, when Tessa was sick, in the hospital. I came in that day with a pile of photos, all the ruins that might have been suited for the Legacy Grant. There were a lot, Harper. Over a dozen places. But you barely looked at any of them." He swallows another mouthful. "You flicked through the pictures as if you didn't really see them. But when you got to the image of this one, you stopped. I remember, because it mattered so much to me that whatever I chose was somewhere you could love too, that you could call home. You touched the photo, but it wasn't the house that caught your eye." He meets my eyes. "It was the red magnolia tree," he says quietly. "You touched the tree and said you thought this place had something special. You said red magnolia trees were rare, and the presence of one here made the place special. You even told Tessa about that tree. You never once mentioned the mansion, but you must have talked about that tree a dozen times. You even told the nurse about it, about how much you loved red magnolias. I didn't think anything of it, then. But now, it's different." He swallows more beer, holding my eyes. "I don't think it was me who chose this mansion, Harper.

"I think it was you.

"I think this place was always meant to be yours. I think you belong to the earth here as much as it belongs to you. I don't think it was my destiny to restore the Marigny mansion. I think the mansion was calling you home—and something in you heard it."

CHAPTER 21

ALONE

Connor holds my eyes after he finishes speaking. I don't know what to say. I do remember the photo, but only vaguely. It's lost in the heartache of Tessa's illness.

"If I remember that at all," I say, "it's that I wanted to like something for your sake. If I really did point this place out, it wasn't because I felt a connection. It was because I was so happy you had a direction to follow, something to give us both hope."

"The first day we visited," Connor goes on as if I hadn't spoken, "it was winter, just like it is now. There were no flowers on the red magnolia. They weren't due for months. There wasn't so much as a bud on the branch. And yet, when I drove back a week later to meet with the realtor, the entire tree was full of blooms. I remember it clearly, because the realtor commented on how odd it was, especially since it was just that one tree, Harper. No other. Just that one."

Reluctantly, I remember the red magnolia outside the church where I married Antoine, the way it had been covered in a deep, beautiful haze of flowers, despite the lateness of the season.

"It's true that you always loved gardening," he says. "But not like you have here. It was always painting first, gardening second. But since we moved here, it's as if you know exactly how and where everything should go, how to make it grow. Yet you've never bought so much as a seed from a store. It's as if you just coaxed the plants back, after a long sleep. Like you brought the garden back to life."

"What are you trying to say, Connor?" I stand up and walk over to him. "Cass said all of this is my fault. What she is, what you've become. Do you feel that way, too?"

"Maybe, a little." He swallows the rest of the beer and throws the empty bottle into the bin by the stairs with unerring accuracy. It makes a loud smash as it shatters on the others there. I flinch. Connor smiles without humor. "But I'm not angry with you, Harper. I can't be. You gave me what I asked for, and I got Cass back. I'm grateful."

"Then what?" I touch his arm. "What can I do to make this better, Connor?"

He looks down at my hand on his arm. He doesn't pull away, but he doesn't reach for it, either.

"I can't live here anymore," he says. "I rented a cabin out by the bayou, near Remy and the other wolves. I belong on their side of the river now, not here. Not on Marigny land." He looks around in distaste. "You don't know how it feels here, for a wolf, Harper. As if there's poison in the ground."

"Poison." His words hurt as effectively as if he'd struck me. "My poison, you mean. Whatever I am." Connor doesn't react to my flat tone.

"I don't know if it's you, or simply the magic they used to bind Keziah here. All I know is that when I'm here, I can feel it, like an itch under my skin. I can't sleep, or relax, here."

"What will you do with the mansion, then? With the project?" I'm struggling to keep my voice steady.

"I'll work on it during the day. I made a commitment to complete it, and I will. But I won't be living here anymore. Cass wouldn't like it, anyway. She finds it hard, being around humans —especially you, Harper."

"Why? Because of my so-called magic? Magic I don't even understand?" I'm hurt and angry, and it's beginning to show. "You're my brother, Connor. The only family I have left."

"But that's just it, Harper." Connor's eyes are dark. "I'm not your brother. I never was. I was just someone who shared your life for a time. I have more in common with Remy and the wolves than I do with you. It's their blood that runs in my veins now. I can hear them, and they listen to me. We're connected in a way you and I never could be."

Every word hurts me like a hammer blow. I struggle to keep my voice calm. "And Cass, Connor? Is she family too, even though she's a vampire?"

"Cass and I are bound." He says it the same way Cass did, as if something links them that goes beyond anything I can understand. "I'm all she has now. All that binds her to life, to her emotions."

"And what about you? What does Cass mean to you?"

"Cass is my soul," Connor says quietly. "The one who unlocked the wolf inside me. She knows me in a way nobody else ever can, not even you, Harper. With her, I know who I am. Without her I'm not whole."

"So that's it?" It's hard to keep from sounding like a petulant child. "All that bound us as family, gone, just like that. You'll finish the Legacy project, then walk away, is that right? To be with Cass, and the wolves. Are you immortal, too? Will you and Cass live in your bound little world forever now, just the two of you?"

"No." Connor's face darkens. "I'm not immortal, Harper, just as you aren't immortal. But you married Antoine anyway. And I will be with Cass. For as long as that is possible for us both."

"And what about us?" I whisper, searching my brother's face. "What will we be, Connor?"

He gives me a small smile, but it doesn't reach his eyes, and there is none of our old companionship in his expression. "We will be what we always should have been. Two people who once shared a home, a period of life together. Who care about each other and catch up, sometimes, for a dinner, but who get on with their separate lives. You've got my phone number. If you need me to sign a form or meet a teacher, you can let me know. Although, since your vampire husband managed to compel his way around my power of attorney in relation to this house, and presumably any other number of officials to ensure your marriage, I'm guessing you don't really need my help anymore."

"I'm sorry, Connor." I search his face. "I'm truly sorry I didn't tell you about my marriage. About everything that's happened since."

"I know you are, Harper." There is no hint of softening in his face. "But the fact is that you didn't. And now everything is different, and I can't make it go back to the way it was. I'm not the Connor you knew anymore, just as Cass isn't the friend you knew. We're changed. We were both *forced* to change, Harper. As a result of the secret you kept hidden under our house. I may understand the choices you make. I may even forgive you for what's happened as a result of them. And I know that whatever power you have isn't your fault." He opens the door of his truck and leans over it, holding my eyes. "But all the understanding in the world doesn't alter the fact that Cass and I are changed forever, because of you and Antoine. Because you chose each other over everyone else. And no matter how much I once cared about you, I can't just forget that, Harper. I'm a wolf now. I have more to worry about than a stepsister who already has a vampire—two vampires, if you count Tate—dedicated to her protection."

Not since we were small children has Connor ever referred to me as a "step" sister. Long ago, when Mom was first sick, a supercilious doctor questioned Connor's right to care for his "stepsisters." Connor had faced the man down with a black glare and said, in the most hostile tone I'd ever heard: *"There's no such thing as steps in this family."*

And yet now, suddenly I am no longer his sister, but a step.

It hurts.

"Will I see you?" My voice rasps painfully in my throat. It's all I can do not to throw myself on his truck and stop him leaving.

"Sometimes, I guess. But I'll do my best to stay out of your way, for a time." Connor swings himself into the truck and for a moment, the interior light shows the hard, angled planes of his face, a man different to the one who has been my brother through so much. "And stay away from Cass, Harper. She has enough to deal with for now without trying to stop herself from drinking your blood, too."

"Drinking my blood?" I say, bewildered. But I'm talking to the air. Connor is gone.

I stand outside the mansion, tears falling in a river down my face, watching the night until the last of his taillights have gone and the sound of the engine has been swallowed by the darkness, more alone than I have ever felt in my life.

CHAPTER 22

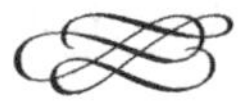

HOPE

I'm still sitting in the dark when Antoine finally arrives. It's the first time I've ever seen him look weary.

"It's done." He walks slowly up the steps. "Nobody will remember what happened at the ball. And Selena's funeral will be held two days from now." He passes a hand over his face and leans against the column. "You should go inside. It's cooled right down out here."

"I can't face it inside." I roll an empty teacup between my hands as I tell him, in halting sentences, what happened between Connor and me. "He won't forgive me," I finish. "Not any time soon."

For once, Antoine doesn't argue. He just comes and sits beside me. I lean my head on his shoulder and we sit quietly, looking out into the still night. Somewhere in the distance, a horned owl cries. The sound is haunting and lonely, like the dark, empty mansion behind me. Antoine's head rests on mine, a quiet comfort. Without moving, I say, "It's time you told me the truth, Antoine. Everything you know about what I am. What this all means." He raises his head and I lift mine. We look at one another. "Everyone seems to know things I don't," I say quietly. "I know you want to protect me. But now I've lost my brother. My best friend. People are dead, Antoine. I need to know what I am."

He nods. Reaching down behind the gardenia, he withdraws a bottle of aged whiskey and smiles wryly at me. "No offense to Connor's rum collection, but Tate and I have rather more expensive taste."

I raise my eyebrows as he pours whiskey into my chipped teacup. "Oh, I see the sophistication. How many of those are stashed around the place?"

He taps his nose. "Some secrets shouldn't be known." He sees my face, and his smile fades. "I didn't keep secrets because I wanted to hide things from you, Harper. I simply didn't know."

"Well," I say, turning to face him, "when, exactly, did you know?"

He tosses off the cup of whiskey and pours himself another one. "The first time I knew for certain that something was — different—about you, was after I drank your blood."

"Why?"

"At first, I thought it was just the way I felt about you. Often that confuses how humans taste to us." He glances at me quickly as if to assess how I react to this. When I don't look away, he goes on: "The longer we desire someone, crave them, often the sweeter the moment when finally we take their blood. Initially, I thought it was simply the way I felt about you that made your blood so potent to me."

Part of me wants to take that line, hold it close and savor it, but what I need to know is more important. "What changed?"

"On the night I drank from you in the tunnels, I ran for hundreds of miles after I left, barely thinking. At first I didn't much care where I was going. I just needed to move, to put distance between you and me, and the memory of the danger I'd put you in. But when dawn came, I became aware that something was different. It wasn't just how I felt emotionally or what had happened. My body felt different. It was as the sun rose that I noticed it—a certain way of reacting to the sun, strange sensations so long forgotten to me that at first I questioned what I felt. But as the day grew, it became unmistakable."

I shake my head. "I don't understand. What kind of sensations?"

The cup dangles between his hands as he turns his head to meet my eyes. "I felt like I was alive again," he says quietly. "I felt as if I were human, Harper."

I stare at him. "How—what's the difference?"

He looks back out down the driveway, the long tunnel of live oak. "You need to understand how it is to be what I am," he says. "What vampires are. We feel so much more than we ever did as humans. Every nerve, every sense, is alert and alive. We are faster, stronger, and keener than any human could ever feel. At first the sensations are overwhelming. That's why Cass suffers so much, at the moment. The smallest sound, the faintest touch or scent, assaults us with unimaginable power. It's both exhilarating and terrifying. It seems that we are more, that everything is more. And at the beginning we confuse that with thinking we are somehow more human than we were before." His mouth tightens. "But over time," he says slowly, "we begin to realize it is the opposite—that we are, quite profoundly, *not* human. At first it is the small things—the lack of normal bodily functions, although we tend to see that as a definite bonus. Our bodies can absorb any amount of food or liquid and break them down to nothing. They neither sustain us nor harm us—they just dissolve, as if they never were. It's why you rarely see us show any sign of inebriation. For a vampire to be drunk, we would have to virtually mainline pure alcohol. At most we might buzz a little, but that's about it." He finishes the whiskey and pours another, raising it in wry salute. "In itself, that is a huge adjustment. To no longer need anything, to be aware of heat and cold, but to be unaffected by them; to observe food, but not feel hunger; to know one has run a hundred miles, yet feel no exhaustion—all of these things are a slow process of realization. Some of us spend decades adjusting only to that. And then there is the bloodlust."

He pauses and glances at me, again assessing my reaction. When I meet his eyes steadily, he continues. "Our need for blood slowly changes the way we see humans. At first it may just be the savage, inhuman lust for blood, as it was for Cass when she turned. But with time it deepens into something else. A kind of cold contempt. A separation. Humans become more animal to us than anything else. Their lives are brief, transient. Emotional attachment becomes impossible. In fifty years, give or take, of being a vampire, we watch every human we ever cared about die. Long before that, we have to accept that they can have no place in our lives. Many of us turn away from humans at the earliest opportunity, the moment we realize there is no path back to our humanity. The pain is too great. And it's more than that. We're designed to see humans as prey. We're a profoundly different species to what we were when alive. The problem is, we don't truly notice the differences. We still feel like *us*—just more, as I said. So while we are aware that we are different to what we were, eventually we forget how it felt to be human, so we couldn't say exactly how we are different.

"But that dawn, after drinking your blood—suddenly, I remembered." The cup dangles forgotten between his large hands, and he stares into the distance, unseeing. "I felt something inside me grow again, like a—long forgotten seed, pushing through frozen soil." He smiles ruefully. "Poetry is not my strength," he says, "but I can't think of a way to describe it other than to say I realized that all this time I had thought myself *more*, I had in fact been less. I had been dead. And I felt alive again. Your blood, coursing through my own, was more potent than any draught of human blood I had taken in three centuries. Not because it tasted like nectar—though it did." Despite his efforts at self-restraint, I see a flash of crimson in his eyes at the memory. I barely suppress a shiver. He nods grimly. "You can't imagine how the memory of it tortured me. I'm ashamed of it even now. But it wasn't the taste, Harper. It was as if your blood was rain after a long drought. It flowed into the cells of my own, if cells they are. Brought them to life again." He takes my hands. "I lay down in the warm grass of a meadow that morning, Harper. As the sun rose, I closed my eyes. Do you know what I saw behind them?"

I shake my head, wanting to know yet frightened to ask.

"In my mind it was as if my body was a garden, one richer and more beautiful than any I had seen before. I could see your blood flowing into it, but it wasn't red, as blood is. It was bright and rich as white gold. Like a river, it flowed to different points along my body, and from them it seemed as if fountains burst into life, one after another, each a different color of the rainbow. It was as if something switched on inside me. Suddenly I could remember exactly how it felt to be alive, and in love, to know that brief, terrifying euphoria, the fear and longing of human love and emotion. But it was something more. It was hope, Harper."

He shakes his head at my frown. "I'm explaining it badly, but that is what I realized, in that moment. Humans have hope. It is perhaps the most brutal thing, but also the bravest. To dare to hope is what it means to be alive. When we die, Harper, we lose that. Hope dies with our humanity.

"Vampires are many things. We might acquire a deal of philosophical wisdom. We can become kind or evil, and often, sadly, both at once. We can acquire skills and knowledge, money and prestige. But hope, Harper"—he looks at me—"hope dies with our human life, for hope belongs to those things that are natural, that live and die a finite existence, and have urgent dreams.

"That morning, I lay in the grass and felt the sun on my body, and I felt hope for the first time in three hundred years." His eyes are cobalt, the gold hard and blazing in their depths. "It terrified me," he says softly. "It scared me more than anything else has in all my existence."

CHAPTER 23

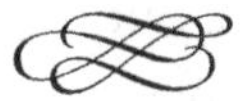

PERFUME

His hands twine in mine, cool and strong, and I look down at them, his skin dark in contrast to my own. My hair falls forward, and he takes one of his hands away and smooths it back from my face. "Say something," he says quietly.

"So this power I have—it's hope?" I raise a shoulder, feeling idiotic. "I guess I don't understand."

"At first, neither did I." Antoine strokes my face. "It's why I said nothing. I didn't understand it, and any explanation I could think of seemed so far-fetched as to be insane. Then I met Noya."

"Noya understood this?"

He nods. "Noya was sick, as you know. She'd been sick for a long time. She was also very connected to her ancestry and natural medicine. She'd done a lot of searching, and in doing so, she'd learned about our kind, about Keziah and Caleb. Perhaps she didn't truly believe it until she met me, but she had the knowledge, at least. More knowledge than I had, as it turned out. It was she who advised me that if I wished to understand what had happened, I would need to contact the medicine woman inside me."

He looks away, then back. "You need to know that I've spent most of these past centuries trying to drown out that part of myself, just as I'd tried to forget Tate. Both connected me to my humanity, to the part that the vampire in me wanted to extinguish. Both had once driven me almost insane. I put them away in a carefully locked box inside myself, one I was more terrified than I care to admit to open. But I did, Harper. I went to a place I used to hunt, long ago, a place that was familiar to Atsila, as well as to myself. I mixed certain herbs, skills I know not from my human life, but from her wisdom. Then I lay down under the stars and asked her to show me the truth of what I'd felt: the truth of what you are."

"What did she say?" It's hard to get the words out.

"She showed me the same garden I'd seen in the meadow. Then it changed, became this place, the land behind the mansion, where you've made a night garden. I saw the red magnolias. She showed me the one outside the church where we married." He grips my hands harder. "Harper, I've known that church from the day it was built. I've visited it maybe every decade or so. There has never been a red magnolia at the door. I swear it wasn't there before the day I decided I wanted to marry you and chose that place to do it. And here, at the mansion itself —when first you came here, there was one red magnolia tree. That one, where your Mustang is always parked." He nods at my convertible. "Now a dozen grow by the slope to the river, and all are in bloom, Harper. Even in the middle of winter."

"But what does it mean? What am I?"

"There are different names for it, in different cultures. In Natchez lore it is different than in Western mythology. The Natchez don't separate themselves from other life-forms. They accept that the spirit of the land may live within a person, just as the spirit of an animal, like a wolf, can be part of a person. Once, people in our culture believed the same, had names for such spirits: dryads, nymphs. The spirits of land, of water. People made places of worship where those spirits were found, at waterfalls, ponds, beneath trees. Sacred places in nature were understood to be where spirits appeared to people. Tree spirits, or dryads, were usually described as beautiful young girls—with wild, untamed hair." He touches the explosion of curls that hangs down my back.

"Then that's what I am? A—dryad?" It seems ridiculous even saying it.

"Not exactly. The dryads of legend could not live separately from their places, their trees. Yet you have lived in a city, far from this place. And you live as a human, not as part of the magnolia tree itself. But somehow there is an essence within you that is linked to this place, to the red magnolia and the earth in which it grows—and whatever that essence is, it has become infinitely more powerful since you came here."

"Connor said it was me who chose this place." I hold Antoine's hands as if they are an anchor, but I can't look at him. "As if I knew I had to come here. And since I have, everything in me seems to have come alive. I thought it was just you. The way I felt about you. Finally having a new life, after Tessa, Mom—after all that death. But Connor reminded me that I never even bought a seed for that night garden. Much as I hate to admit it, Antoine, he's right. I never consciously thought about that garden. It just—grew. Some nights all I did was sit beside it and dream of what it could be. I don't recall so much as learning the names of the plants that grow in it. One day it was simply there, and I seemed to know how to tend it. The only seeds I recall actually planting are the night jasmine that my sister gave me."

He nods. "Somehow you belong to this earth. You become stronger upon it, and it becomes more magical with every day you tend it."

"But why is that so dangerous? Why is it that Cass hates me so much, and Connor keeps his distance?"

Antoine rises abruptly and moves away from me, standing

with his hands loosely on his hips, sideways to me, so I can't read his face except in profile. "What I'm about to tell you is all I know, and it's more than anyone else does, no matter what they say. I know it partly from the medicine woman, and partly from Keziah—but mostly I know it because I drank your blood. I know it in a way nobody else can, unless they do that." He turns to face me. "And they mustn't, Harper," he says fiercely. "You have to promise me that you will never let any of our kind drink from you again. Including me."

"Okay," I say slowly. "I promise. But you need to explain why."

"I drank less than a pint of your blood," he says. " I wanted more, believe me. But I forced myself to stop." He pulls me to my feet and holds my hands and eyes as he speaks. "Harper—less than half a pint of your blood was enough to cut through my immortality for more than an entire day. In that time, my body began to repair itself, to have life flow through it again. It was euphoria more than any I have known in three hundred years." He grips my hands hard. "A sensation vampires would kill for, Harper, without a second thought, if it should become known. And there is more."

"What more could there possibly be?" I mutter.

"You saw what my blood did to the wolves."

"It activated them," I say, remembering what Remy had said the morning after they were turned. Antoine nods.

"The medicine woman inside me," he says, "she showed me that, too. She herself was part of nature, held earth magic and knowledge in her veins. It's a powerful force, Harper. More powerful than perhaps any other magic there is. The force of the earth itself, of rivers and wind, of earthquakes and volcanoes. It is an unlimited source. I possess only a trace of it, the memory of her spirit. I knew vampire blood had magical properties—for healing, for example. But mine is different. Mine can trigger changes such as that which made Remy and your brother wolves." He grips my hands, looking at me intently. "But your brother became more than a wolf, Harper. He became the most powerful wolf of the whole clan, more powerful than Remy himself. Do you know why that is?"

"I'm guessing it's something to do with me."

He nods. "The mixture you made for him to drink," he says. "It was imbued with your spirit, your power. When your brother drank it, he took part of that inside himself—just as my blood gave him more of the same. He's not just a wolf, Harper. He's probably the most powerful wolf ever to live." He pauses.

"What is it? What aren't you saying?"

"Keziah knows what you are." He shakes his head in frustration. "And whatever it is, she is wary of it. She should have drunk from you - but she hasn't. There's something we aren't seeing, and it makes me uneasy."

He glances at me. "Do you remember what happened to Caleb that night?"

I nod. "I could feel him, in the earth, under my feet."

"I told you once that Keziah is the strongest of our kind I've ever met." He is still holding my hands, and he presses them, drawing me closer to him. "After speaking to Cass, Tate and I both think that perhaps it was Caleb all along who was the true strength. That he, too, had power connected to the earth, power than enabled Keziah to survive burning, power imbued in the totems they both wore. We think that is why Keziah might have turned him to begin with. To gain access to his power, use it for herself."

"That's what she meant." I release his hands and stand up, unable to sit still. "When she said you had access to all that power."

"Exactly. We suspect that she can feel it, inside you. Whatever you are, I think Keziah understands it more than we do. Cass won't say much, but I know her mind is still linked to Keziah's, in a way mine isn't. She knows what you are, too, or at least she feels it, in the blood with which I injected her. Your blood cut through her bond with Keziah, at least enough to give her the strength to resist her Maker."

"Cass said it was Connor who did that, not me. She was very clear."

"She lied," Antoine says flatly. He stands up, brushing the grass from his jeans. "Cass knows it was your blood that separated her from Keziah. She just doesn't want to admit it, to acknowledge the power you have."

"But why does she hate me?"

"She doesn't hate you, Harper. She fears you." I step back from him, surprised.

"Fears me? Cass is a vampire. Why would she fear me?"

"Think about it, Harper." He lifts his shoulders. "Your blood cuts through immortality. It's possible you can actually make a vampire mortal, at least temporarily. And if a vampire is mortal—"

"They can be killed," I breathe.

"Exactly."

We are silent for a moment, while this realization dawns on me.

"If Keziah turned Caleb," I say, "she must have drunk from him."

He nods. "She made Caleb her creature. He was always that way—her shadow, her servant. Whatever power he had, Keziah made it hers, whether by drinking his blood or taking his life, I don't know. But what I do know is that she understands your power. And now that Caleb is gone, Keziah will likely seek to take it for herself. She is already wondering why I have not."

"She knew we had—been together." I flush, remembering the way she looked at me at the ball. "She said, *now that you have taken her*. She said you were ruthless. Why is that?"

Antoine looks away uncomfortably. My eyes narrow. "Antoine? What aren't you telling me?"

"There was a reason I fought against being with you, Harper. And not for all the reasons you thought. Not because I didn't want you—because I do, Harper. I want you more than I've wanted anything in my life, ever." He pulls me against him, his hand broad and strong on my back. "Because after I drank your blood, I feared what my taking your body in that way would do to you. I worried that somehow what I am would trigger something in you, just as my blood did in your brother and the wolves. I feared that if I took you, I would somehow become intoxicated, as I was when I drank your blood. Perhaps I wouldn't be able to stop myself from hurting you; perhaps I would somehow claim your power for my own. I know that's what Keziah believes. Perhaps that is how it was for her and Caleb; I can't know. What I do know is that I was more afraid than I'd ever been before, every time I so much as touched you, that my being with you would destroy you. And I couldn't live with myself, Harper, if that happened. I couldn't bear to be the reason you became something other than what you were born to be. So in the single most difficult decision of my life, I swore I wouldn't do it, no matter how much I wanted to."

"Then why did you?" I whisper, pressing myself against him.

"Because I'm selfish," he mutters. "Because I couldn't bear for you to think I didn't want you. And because despite whatever I told myself, and no matter how wrong I knew it was, I just didn't have the strength to resist you anymore." He pulls back, and the uncertainty in his face makes my heart twist. He strokes my face. "But now that you know it all, I need to ask you again. If you say the word, I will walk away from you now, tonight, and never claim you again, so long as you live. I swear it."

I step closer, and I thrill to see his eyes darken, the last vestiges of control falling away. "You want me," I murmur, my mouth against his ear, and I'm smiling, I can't help it. He groans and gathers me close, lifting me easily so I twine about him, his mouth hungry on mine as he carries me up the stairs, and into the mansion.

"I want you so much I can barely stand being near you," he says against my skin. "I wanted you before I ever tasted your blood, or felt your power, or so much as suspected what you were. I wanted you from the day I first saw you." He cups my face, his eyes dark and searching. "I wanted you from the first," he says, "but I loved you from the day I saw that scar on your side, and knew you'd given part of yourself to save your sister, even though it could cost your own life one day. I loved you when you asked me to marry you—" he grins at my discomfort, but it fades as fast as it came, and his face is serious when he says softly, "and I loved you when we said our vows. I didn't marry you to save the binding. I didn't take your body because of some power neither of us understand. I married you because I love you more than my own existence, and I took you because if I lived one more day without knowing you inside and out, I was going to go insane."

"And now?" I whisper, as he carries me upstairs.

"And now," he says, his mouth restless and wild against my own, "now you are mine, Harper Marigny, and I am yours. And no matter what comes for us, or what life brings, we are one, now and forever—and we face it together."

Through the open window, the river smells rich and deep. The last of the wolf's moon dies in a thin crescent, the night sky black as ink, and far below us, the flowers of the night garden open, spreading their secrets in a dangerous perfume on the still night air.

EPILOGUE

Dear Tessa,

They say that marriage is built upon honesty. I believe that. But I also believe that sometimes, not everything has to be said.

When she was talking about her bond with Connor, there was something Cass said that stuck in my mind: *He holds me in his blood.*

She said his blood anchors her. *His blood,* she said to me. *Not yours, Harper.*

But it *is* my blood. It was my blood that made Connor, and my blood that broke the bond between Cass and Keziah.

I haven't told anyone about the night I made Connor's potion, how I cut my finger on the knife. The blood from my finger was all over the wolfsbane leaves. I remember the potion, how it had a deep indigo sheen. That indigo came from my blood. Don't ask me how I know that. I just do. I know it deep inside. In my veins.

Before Antoine gave Remy and the other bayou men his blood, he had drunk from me. Perhaps he is right, and it really is the medicine woman inside him that activated the wolves. But I'm not so sure.

I think I activated the wolves.

Connor has no idea. Connor thinks he has more in common with the wolves, now, than he does with me.

Cass only remembers that Connor bit her. She thinks it's Connor's blood that affected her, but it's not—it's mine. Somewhere inside herself, Cass knows that, and secretly resents it.

I don't think Connor knows it the same way.

The truth is that it is my blood that runs through his veins. We truly are joined now.

But I have not said that. I haven't said it to anyone.

Whatever I am, I don't want it to hurt anyone more than it already has. If my blood can make a man a wolf, can break the bond between a vampire and her Maker—what else might it do?

I can't think about it, Tessa. I don't want to.

What I want is to lose myself, just for a time, in this love.

Something Antoine said has stayed with me: T*o dare to hope is what it means to be alive.*

Hope is, as he said, perhaps the most brutal thing—but also the bravest.

So that is what I will do, Tessa. In this supernatural world I find myself part of, there is little I can control. Even the blood in my veins, it seems, has powers beyond my understanding. But I can hope. Hope that somehow, my brother and Cass will come back to me. Hope that Keziah doesn't hurt anyone else that I love.

Hope that somehow, against all the odds, Antoine and I find a way to stay together.

And perhaps it will prove to be brutal rather than brave. Maybe hope will be my downfall. Maybe all of this will end in blood, and death.

But I will hope, nonetheless.

Hope is all I have now, Tessa.

. . .

Your twin,
Harper

~

Click here to read Bayou Rose, the next in series, or turn the page to read sample chapters and for your link to Antoine's story, a free prequel novella exclusive to readers.

BAYOU ROSE SAMPLE CHAPTER 1

Dear Tessa,

Spring is here, but inside, I feel as if winter never left.

Connor and Cass remain in the bayou. I know Connor comes here during the day. I see the work he has done, his tools where he left them. But he waits until I am at school to arrive and is gone when I get home. Once I came home early, just to try to catch him, but our brother is a wolf now. He was gone before I parked under the magnolia.

Antoine goes quiet when I ask about Connor. He's tried to reason with him, I'm guessing. I could have told him it wouldn't work. The brother we knew is gone now, lost in his wolf's body and his love for Cass. I wish I could simply let him go as easily as it seems he has me. But I miss him. I miss them both. Connor is all that is left of us, Tessa, of the family we once were together. Losing him feels like someone cut a part of me away without anesthetic. Antoine does his best to fill that space, but even he cannot take the pain away, though I love him so much that I sometimes feel guilty—for being so happy when you are dead, and Connor is gone.

It's all so confusing.

Antoine makes me go to school. I know Mom wanted us to get our high school diplomas, and to honor her memory I'm doing my best to complete senior year, but I think we all knew I was never the college type. Without Cass, and with Keziah's shadow lurking just out of sight, school feels as cold as the mansion does with no Connor inside it. Even Avery is more distant. She spends more time with Remy than with me, now, and there seems to be a hard edge to her voice sometimes when she talks about Connor. I think his leadership of the wolves has caused some problems, though she doesn't tell me anything, and at times I feel like she blames me for all of it. We aren't friends in the same way we were before all of this.

Jeremiah and I have become increasingly close at school. He spends as much time at the mansion as he does at the house he and Antoine supposedly share, though Antoine hasn't spent a night there in weeks now.

I'd be lying if I said that last sentence didn't make my stomach flip a little. But I can almost see you rolling your eyes at me, so I won't talk about the nights. I'm not sure I'd have the words, anyhow.

Antoine and I don't talk about my so-called powers, whatever they are. It's the one subject that we both stay away from. So do Tate and Jeremiah. I figure that's Antoine's doing. I know he's worried. If I'm honest, Tessa, I'm worried too, and not just for myself.

Antoine doesn't say anything, but I suspect Keziah is calling him again. He seems so grim sometimes, like there's a battle going on inside him. At first I thought it was only my imagination. Then Avery let something slip in class one day that made me think Cass is struggling, too. Keziah is still out there, waiting, preying on us all. It's like we're living in the interval between acts in a play, waiting for the curtain to go up and show us the next scene.

It's an uneasy interlude.

I've filled it by starting a water garden. I know you probably think I should just stop growing anything, but I can't help it. Planting is the only thing that helps the loneliness go away. The night garden is riotous and full, but since Connor became a wolf, I can't bear being in it. The water garden is sunlit joy, a peaceful little pond just above a curve of the river, where I have planted bulbs of lilies and lotus. They're still hiding beneath the murky surface, but when they bloom, they should come up as a beautiful sea of light yellow and blue, like a reflection of the sun and sky.

I feel as if we all need as much sunlight and joy as I can create.

I'm writing this down on the jetty. I painted today: a lotus, just like those I've planted. It made me feel warm inside. It's the first painting I've done in forever, and I'm actually proud of it. I think I will hang it in my bedroom, to remind me that even when I feel like winter will never leave my heart, there is always sunshine, somewhere. No matter how dark and tough he is, I think our brother needs that sunlight too. He needs us, Tessa. Maybe even more than we ever needed him. But I don't know how to bridge the gap.

I love you so much, Tessa. I'm glad I buried your ashes here. I feel you, in the whisper of wind and the soft, slow movement of the river. I know you are always with me.

If you have any power over there, wherever you are, I hope you are whispering to Connor, too.

Your twin,
Harper

BAYOU ROSE SAMPLE CHAPTER 2

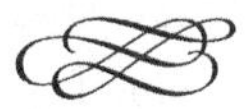

It's late afternoon on a Sunday, and puff clouds drift across a dreamy spring sky. The river is moving slowly, and I'm knee-deep in it, feeling for the water lily and lotus bulbs in the rich silt below. The scent of wildflowers mixes with apricot on a soft breeze, and for a time at least, I can forget that my brother is no longer family, and that a vampire who wants me dead is still on the loose.

"You look like a hobo."

I smile without turning around. "Gardening is hardly a fashion event."

"Gardening." I can hear the amusement in Antoine's voice. It makes my stomach curl in a slow, warm feeling. "In a hat that is more brim than anything else, a pair of shorts barely worthy of the name, and a bikini top? You should definitely garden more often."

"And boots," I say in my defense.

"Let us not forget the boots." I turn around to find him leaning against the red magnolia that hangs over the water garden, arms folded, regarding me with hooded eyes and a lazy smile that makes my pulse race. I know that look.

"I probably smell like river water," I say, backing away. But he's fast, too fast, and before I finish speaking, he has lifted me up and placed me on the red magnolia branch, one hand resting on the base of my spine, the other splayed on the trunk beside me.

"I don't know." He leans in so his lips are at the soft part behind my jaw. "You smell like springtime," he murmurs, and then my arms are around his neck and for the next while, even my lotus bulbs are forgotten.

"We should go in," I whisper a while later. "It's getting cool out."

"Is that right?" he gathers me closer. "I hadn't noticed."

"Dinner," I begin weakly.

"Can be ordered in."

"Jeremiah—"

"Is at the river house."

He kisses me again, and it's hard to so much as think, let alone speak, and I vaguely wonder why I am arguing. Just as I'm giving in to the idea that dinner might end up being pizza, I feel him tense against me. He turns to look out over the river, and in the golden sunlight full of bugs and river haze, his eyes are steel grey and somehow distant, as if he's gone somewhere I can't follow.

"Antoine?" I say uncertainly. His arms are still around me, but the warm intimacy of moments ago is gone, replaced by cold detachment. "Antoine?" I repeat, more concerned this time. A moment later he turns back to me, his eyes snapping into focus, as if he's just remembered where he is.

"Dinner." His voice is strained, and the smile he gives me doesn't reach his eyes. "Maybe we should have something healthy, after all." He gives me the same forced smile and lifts me easily off the branch, carefully brushing the scraps of bark from my legs, but managing to avoid my eyes.

"What's wrong?" I ask bluntly.

"Nothing. I think a cloud passed over the sun. You're right—it's getting cool out." He turns away and starts collecting my gardening tools. I stare at his back, but he doesn't offer anything more, and I let it go, for now.

A while later I've washed the river off, night has fallen, and Antoine is grilling steaks on the porch while I toss a salad. Despite all the work Connor has done on the mansion, the makeshift kitchen that opens onto the front porch is still where we spend most of our time. I know it will be renovated soon, returned to the parlor it once was, but it's the only room in the mansion other than my bedroom that really feels like home. If I'm honest, it also feels like Connor, and when I'm here, it's as if he still is, too, in the comforting remnants of our old existence—the beer stein I once gave him on top of the icebox that I've kept even though we have a refrigerator now, and his tools lying about on the shelf.

"He'll find his way back, in time." I turn to find Antoine watching me, his eyes dark. I know he worries about Connor and me. He knows how much I love my brother. Right now, though, Connor isn't the one on my mind, for once.

"What happened earlier?" I'm directly facing him, so I see the opaque veil that falls over his eyes as I ask the question. "It's her, isn't it," I say when he doesn't answer. "Keziah."

His arms are folded and he's leaning against the doorframe, the steaks lying forgotten on a plate on the sideboard. There is a faint crease between his brows, and he looks away evasively. "I can tell." I try and fail to find his eyes. "I remember how it was, with Cass and Avery."

"It isn't the same." His response is clipped and hard, but it doesn't deter me.

"If she's trying to get into your head, there is a way we can make sure we keep her out."

The crease between his brows deepens in momentary confusion. Then his eyes widen, and he almost shudders with distaste as he realizes what I'm suggesting. "I told you once before that I'd never drink your blood again," he says curtly. "I meant it, Harper. Don't ever suggest that. Don't even think it."

"Why not?" I fold my own arms and lean against the table, glaring at him. "It's the one thing we know works. Until we find a way to . . . end her, it might be the only way to keep you safe." I can't quite bring myself to say the word *kill*. Is it really killing, when the creature is Keziah, an ancient being that is something even more dead—and deadly—than a vampire?

Antoine opens his mouth for what I know is going to be a fierce rejoinder but, seeing my face, sighs and rubs a large hand over his face and around the back of his neck. "I know you mean well." I can tell how hard it is for him to keep an even tone. "But you can't begin to imagine how repugnant I find the thought of using you to fight Keziah. Of taking your blood as my own shield." He meets my eyes, cavernous darkness in his own. "Can you understand that?"

"I understand that you are proud." I step forward and put my hands on his face. "That you don't want to admit weakness. But have you considered that you might be the only one who can protect me? What happens if you don't take my blood, and Keziah gets into your head?"

For a moment I see shadows shift in the darkness, and I think it's worked, that he will listen to me. Then he covers my hands with his own and shakes his head, smiling ruefully as he brings our clasped hands down between us. "Good try," he says wryly. "You almost had me there."

"It's true," I insist, but I know the moment has passed.

"Harper." He puts his arms around me so they rest loosely at the base of my spine. "If I start drinking from you—where does it stop? *When* does it stop? And what if it is hurting you somehow, or binding you to me in a way that could be used against you?" He shakes his head. "Whatever runs through your veins, it isn't normal human blood. It's something so potent it contains the force of the earth, of water. It's magical." He smiles crookedly. "But when it's in my system, it's also all I can think about. And right now, I don't want to think about your blood, Harper. I just want to be with you." He pulls me closer, his lips hot and disturbing against mine. "I want to be with you so much I can barely think of anything else," he murmurs, and now my arms are about his neck, and when he pushes the steaks to one side and lifts me onto the sideboard, food is the last thing on my mind. "I won't drink from you," he says against my mouth, his hands twining in my hair. "But I will protect you, Harper. I swear it. If you believe nothing else—believe that."

And then there is nothing but heat and the wild night, and dinner winds up as cold steak and salad, a long time later.

BAYOU ROSE SAMPLE CHAPTER 3

For all that Antoine denies it, Keziah's calls weigh him down. He spends more time at the river house, making the excuse that I need to focus on studying for finals, which are barely weeks away. He shies away from any mention of Keziah's name.

Keziah herself doesn't come to school anymore, a small mercy for which I should probably be grateful, but instead makes me uneasy. Without regular contact with the wolves, I'm unsure of her whereabouts, though occasional rumors of increased death rates in the small bayou settlements do reach Deepwater from time to time. I wish I could ask Remy or Avery. But Remy and the wolves are in the bayou with my brother, as lost to me as he is. Avery spends all her available time with Remy. Going by the way he almost consumes her when he collects her in the parking lot from school, there is clearly no confusion about their relationship anymore. I feel sorry for Jeremiah. He never says anything, but I see him watching Avery with Remy, and I know it must hurt. I think he misses her friendship as much as anything else. I know how he feels. With Cass in the bayou cabin with Connor, and Avery immersing herself in Natchez law with Remy and his mom, Lori, it's just Jeremiah and me.

"Have you noticed anything off about Antoine lately?" Jeremiah asks me abruptly one morning as we are walking toward class. The sky shimmers with May heat and the aftermath of an overnight storm. Summer is almost here, school almost over. I've already submitted my artwork. These last weeks feel like the calm before real life begins, whatever that looks like for me.

I take my time before I answer him. "Like what?" I say, careful to keep a neutral tone. Jeremiah stops just beyond the school doors and faces me.

"Last night I couldn't sleep," he says. "I came downstairs to get a drink, and Antoine was standing at the glass doors that face onto the river. They were all open wide, even though it was a windy night, with lightning in the sky."

"He likes storms," I say unconvincingly. "Especially the summer electrical ones."

"We all like watching the summer storms, Harper," snaps Jeremiah. "But we don't generally stand still as a statue while rain pounds in through open doors."

I suppress a faint shudder. There is something about the image his words conjure up that makes me feel as if the storm is still here, all around me. "So what is it that you're trying to say?" I know my question sounds defensive, but I also don't have answers.

"I think Keziah is calling him again." Jeremiah shoots me an almost apologetic glance.

"She is," I say flatly.

"You already knew?"

"I knew." I try to smile at him. "We talked about it."

"If Keziah is calling him, don't you think we should be doing a little more than talking about it? What if he can't fight her off?"

"I know, Jeremiah, okay?" I interrupt his indignant flow. The steps have almost cleared, and we're about to be late for class. "Antoine says he can handle it. And he won't accept what help I can offer."

"You mean—" Jeremiah looks around and lowers his voice. "Your blood?"

"Yes, my blood." I meet his eyes. "Antoine won't drink it."

"Why not?"

"Because," says a third voice which makes us both spin around, "Antoine has always fought his battles alone." Tate has materialized at our side. With his long hair tied back, wearing jeans and a faded plaid shirt, he looks less the history teacher he is impersonating and more like an ad for an outdoor magazine. "Taking Harper's blood would be admitting weakness. It would go against every moral code to which Antoine has ever held himself."

"Moral codes won't help any if he winds up Keziah's slave again," says Jeremiah, clearly unmoved by this argument.

"Isn't there something you can do?" I ask Tate. "It's getting worse, I can tell. And he won't talk to me about it."

"He won't speak to me, either." Tate gives me a resigned look. "Although I'm not sure why I thought he would, given he hasn't confided in me for the past three centuries." He walks past us into school. "Since you're supposed to be in my history class," he says over his shoulder, "you should probably come too."

"Why are you still pretending to be a teacher, anyhow?" Jeremiah mutters to Tate as we go inside. "Keziah's not coming to class anymore."

"She could return at any time. Not a chance Antoine or I am prepared to take. And besides," Tate casts us a wry smile, "I enjoy it more than I thought I would."

In fact, Tate is a wonderful teacher. He's so much more engaging than Mr. Larkin, whom he compelled out of the job in winter term, that I know for a fact the school board has already offered him a large raise to stay. I suspect Tate is considering taking it, too. He seems to have slotted into Deepwater life with the diplomacy that is his vampiric gift, charming the women of the Historical and Legacy Societies, enchanting his students, and making himself so helpful to other staff members that even the most conservative and single of the female teachers bat their eyes when he wishes them good morning.

Today the students look up eagerly as he pushes open the classroom door. They are crowded around a tablet which Jared Baudelaire waves eagerly in Tate's direction as we enter. "Mr. Garrison," he says excitedly. "We found something about the tribe in Haiti we were reading about last week."

"The Taíno?" Tate puts his bag down on his desk. His head is down. There's something in his voice, a certain tension, that goes unnoticed by Jared, but makes Jeremiah and I exchange a wary glance.

"Yes, them." Jared points at the tablet. "Apparently, there was a god or something called Macocael, who was supposed to stand guard over a mountain cave during the day. When he left his post, he was punished by being turned to stone. The Taíno worshipped him as a god. They had really cool symbols, called zemis, that they used to represent their gods."

"An impressive, if somewhat sketchy, summary of a very complex indigenous culture," Tate says. He's smiling, but an odd shadow lurks at the back of his eyes, and instead of drawing the conversation out as he normally would, he turns it to a discussion about the impact of colonial settlement on indigenous cultures. The class is interesting, but I notice he steers away from any conversation about the Taíno culture. By the end of the class, Jared seems to have forgotten anything about it.

"This is our last class," says Tate as we are packing up. Everyone pauses and stares at him.

"Why?" Jared is frowning. "We're barely weeks from our final exam. You can't just leave."

"Mr. Larkin will be here to answer any questions you might have." He holds up a hand as a general groan rises from the class. "And I will also be available by phone and email. But to be honest"—he smiles around warmly—"you've all worked very hard, and I think you can look forward to very good results." Despite their desire to look cool, even Jared and the jocks seem appeased by that, going by the bashful looks and mock punches they throw at each other. I wonder if it's only Jeremiah and me who notice that Tate never answered Jared's question.

"So where are you going?" I ask under cover of everyone clattering their chairs.

"I have a project overseas." Tate is looking down at his bag and doesn't meet my eyes.

"To do with the Taíno, that tribe in Haiti?" Jeremiah comes to stand beside me. Tate still doesn't look at us.

"Will this project help Antoine?" I ask. That makes him look up.

"I don't know," he says quietly. "But it may help me understand Keziah. And if I understand her, perhaps, yes, I might find a way to help Antoine—and Cass."

"I thought you said you'd studied mythologies all over the world, researching her?" The room is empty but for the three of us now.

"I have." Tate slings the bag over his shoulder. "But it seems I was looking in the wrong place. Until last week, when our good friend Mr. Baudelaire stumbled across an internet article about the Taíno, and I did some more research." He meets my eyes. "You have to understand," he says with a faint smile, "the last time I researched Caribbean tribes, nobody was discussing the Taíno. Their culture had been hidden from white attention, thought long gone, if thought of at all. And at the time, I was focusing my attention on African cultures." He shrugs. "I just missed it," he says, and I can tell by the crease between his brows that he blames himself for the oversight.

"And now you think there might be some clues there?"

"Perhaps." His expression is guarded. "But you must understand, Harper: I've followed a hundred leads before. This is just as likely to produce nothing more than those did."

"But it might." I can hear the same excitement in Jeremiah's voice that I feel, a glimmer of light at the end of the dark, oppressive tunnel Keziah's existence has cast over our lives.

"It might," Tate concedes reluctantly, turning away. "I have to get to class."

"When are you going?" I call after him.

"I fly from Jackson tonight." The glance he gives me is guarded. "But don't get your hopes up, Harper. I've chased these rainbows before."

Despite Tate's reluctance to feed my optimism, the rest of the day passes in daydreams of a Keziah-free life, one where Antoine's face doesn't go dark and detached with an internal war he won't allow me to help him fight. When I emerge from school to find him waiting in the lot, I feel my heart surge in a way that not even Avery racing away from me with barely a backward glance or so much as a cursory greeting can diminish.

"You look happy." He gives me the twisted smile that always makes my stomach curl. He's leaning against his teal Chevy truck, impossibly handsome in an open linen shirt over faded jeans, showing just enough corded arm muscle that a nearby group of girls cast me an envious glance and erupt into nervous giggles when they pass.

"You shouldn't come to school." I smile as he pulls me close. "You are far too distracting to the student body."

"There's really only one student body I'm interested in," he murmurs, kissing me in a way that has even the conservative female teachers casting me glances of mingled envy and disapproval. He opens the door and I climb into the truck, aware of the curious eyes watching us. I know our relationship separates me from the rest of my class and draws the concern of teachers, many of whom have taken me aside at one time or another to inquire, in their caring but extremely clumsy manner, if I might need to speak to the school counselor. Since what I would have to say would end with me locked in an institution, I've waved off their concerns, but I know they talk about me behind the staff room door. Tate and I have laughed about it, more than once, even though I suspect Tate shares their concerns.

"You're in a good mood." I glance sideways at him as we drive out of town. "Jeremiah said you had a difficult night."

His face tenses. He reaches over and takes my hand, softening his face with a noticeable effort. "Jeremiah shouldn't concern himself."

"He knows what it is, Antoine. We both do. Even Tate knows." He lets go of my hand and stares out the window, his face set and hard once more. "There's no point being angry," I say impatiently. "We just want to help."

"And if I need help," he says tersely, "I will ask for it." I'm opening my mouth to argue when he slams the brakes on, bringing the truck to a sliding halt just beyond the mansion gates.

"What is it?" I peer through the thick branches of the live oak along the driveway.

"There's someone at the mansion." He cocks his head, every sense alert, then relaxes slightly. "Human. A girl, younger than you." He turns to me. "Are you expecting anyone?"

I shake my head. "Not that I know of."

He turns through the gates and we approach the house slowly. Antoine is right. Sitting on the steps is a thin girl with a pointed, pixie-like face and very short black hair. She has wary eyes and clutches a worn duffel bag close to her side as she watches me get out of the truck.

"Hi." I smile at her. "I'm Harper. Were you looking for me?"

"Kind of." She doesn't return my smile but stares instead at Antoine. "Is your name Connor?"

"No." Antoine isn't smiling either. "But perhaps you might like to tell us yours?"

"My name is Callie." The girl clutches her duffel bag protectively. "I'm looking for Connor Ellory. He's my brother."

To continue reading, purchase Bayou Rose here. Turn over for your free prequel novella.

AFTERWORD

If you enjoyed reading Poison Berry, please consider leaving a review on Goodreads or Amazon. Reviews help indie authors more than you can imagine - I can't tell you how much I appreciate them.

You can read Antoine's story, a prequel to the Nightgarden Saga, here. You can also download at www.paulaconstant.com. It is free and exclusive to readers!

You can listen to the music that helped inspire the Nightgarden Saga on this Spotify list.

Follow me on TikTok: @paulaconstant. Tag me in your review, and I will share and promote you!

You can also join the Nightgarden Readers Facebook group, and chat with others (and me) about the series.

If you would like to be the first to read and review advance copies of upcoming books, please visit www.paulaconstant.com and sign up.

To buy any of the books in the series, please go to Amazon.

ABOUT THE AUTHOR

Lucy Holden is a pseudonym for Paula Constant, an Australian author who lives in the gorgeous north western pearling town of Broome. She adores gin martinis, dreaming on the beach beneath a full moon, and having pool book club with awesome friends. The name Lucy is taken from the girl who stepped through the wardrobe in the Narnia books, and Holden refers to Paula's beloved first car.

Paula is the author of historical fiction series the Visigoths of Spain, and travel memoirs Slow Journey South and Sahara.

www.paulaconstant.com

Made in the USA
Las Vegas, NV
14 October 2023